CONTENTS

DEPARTMENTS

FICTION & POETRY

ESSAYS

PICTORIALS

The Act Itself is a new erotica publication featuring exciting short fiction, breathtaking artwork, and informative articles from the world of adult entertainment. Your hostess is known simply as 'The Mrs.' and she works tirelessly to present the very best – all smiles, sighs, and the occasional titter. Our publisher, Bearmanor Media, is a 14-year veteran in publishing fine entertainment books and we're excited to be a part of this new venture.

We will be publishing three times a year – toward the ends of April, August and December, promising 150 pages of goodness in each issue. ***The Act Itself*** will be available via subscription, through order via our publisher, BearManor Media, Amazon, and elsewhere (we'll keep you posted!). Digital and audio options are being examined.

We are currently open to submissions of short fiction and art, open to advertising, and open to nonfiction queries. Check out our guidelines, advertising rates, and subscription pages (in this issue!) for more information.

Oh... and don't forget to look for us on Facebook. Yeah, we'll be there.

The Act Itself
Volume 1, Number 1

For information, address:

BearManor Media
P. O. Box 71426
Albany, GA 31708

theactitself.com

Published in the USA by BearManor Media

ISBN – 1-59393-398-3
978-1-59393-398-2

Welcome

Good moaning. And welcome, to *The Act Itself*. You know what I mean. That thing that rings the wooden world like a doorbell, but we must not call it by its fucking name. Sex. Softcore sex.

This magazine shall explore the wonder that is the R rated sexual experience. Sometimes we'll get a little racy—I myself have been accused of being a true whore in my language, in my literary descriptions and the plethora. But. For the most part, I believe that it's what you can't see and experience that makes the rest of life all the more sexy.

Erotica. Rather than porn.

I was watching *Keeping the Faith* with my hubby just last night, and neither of us could fathom why it mattered during the bedroom scenes that Jenna Elfman had more material surrounding her than she did walking around her office. Which was the more exciting of scenes? I would choose the office. The lines of her hips and the straightness of her tummy; the subtle experience of her breasts pacing up and down in a non-dark shirt. Hubby and I both agreed that lying to hide "it" in the sheets was a lot more hypocritical and a lot less sensuous than that which occurs naturally. *Dharma & Greg* scenes when they're just *talking* is infinitely hotter, to me, than your basic *Basic Instinct*, your Showtime after midnight, and much of what you get in non-plot porn nowadays.

And that's what you'll get here. For the most part. Titillation has a tit in it, don't forget. So does the title of my little winky mag. For anyone who thinks *Goodbye Emmanuelle* is hotter than a Peter North stream, *The Act Itself* is for That Girl. If you're spending your hours watching Tanya Roberts in *Sheena* rather than pumping the gun to *Don't Tell Mom I Ass Fucked the Babysitter #3*, we are here for you.

That is not to say a little Jessica Drake is an evil thing (far from it!). But I do find a lot of the streaming, downloading, "free" porns the boring sort. In and out, no introductions, no apologies, no semblance of truth, honesty, shyness, character (even without a story) or empathy. It is just there. In three holes, five positions, without even trying. Cruising by in a van or setting the girl on her knees immediately. Without the façade of story, desire, something beyond merely picking the prettiest girl to bend over… sameness even of gorgeousness does start to bore.

One must try.

Enjoy the first issue of many!

The Mrs.

AMALGAM

by Lisa Kopel

illustrations by Lee Melton

He slapped my face
lightly at first.
When I didn't flinch-
just looked at him-
harder
then harder still.
Grabbing my hair
snapping back my head
with one hard yank
he pushed himself roughly
into my mouth.
I could have bitten him
vulnerable as he was.
But I didn't.

The pillows so soft
conform to my head
as I lie there
Chianti-tipsy
legs encased
in fishnet tights
body smooth and ready
in the lavender scented
hotel suite
in broken still silence
waiting for you
to get off the phone
with your wife
and come fuck me.

Trot me out like a dog
and I'll perform.
I'll be whatever it is
you want me to be.
Your bad girl your sad girl
it doesn't matter to me.
Dress me up
in black silk and lace
arrange me just so
on the bed.
Tell me that you see God
when I part my lips.
Whisper my name
and I'll answer.

Lisa quietly became Tango about fifteen years ago, and only recently began putting pen to paper, thinking that her exploits and adventures would make a neat book. Lisa lives in Providence, RI and, in addition to having sex, enjoys running, listening to The Beatles and watching reality T.V. Lisa may be contacted at tangostales.com.

LOVE IN SHADOWS

photos by Joseph Giblin

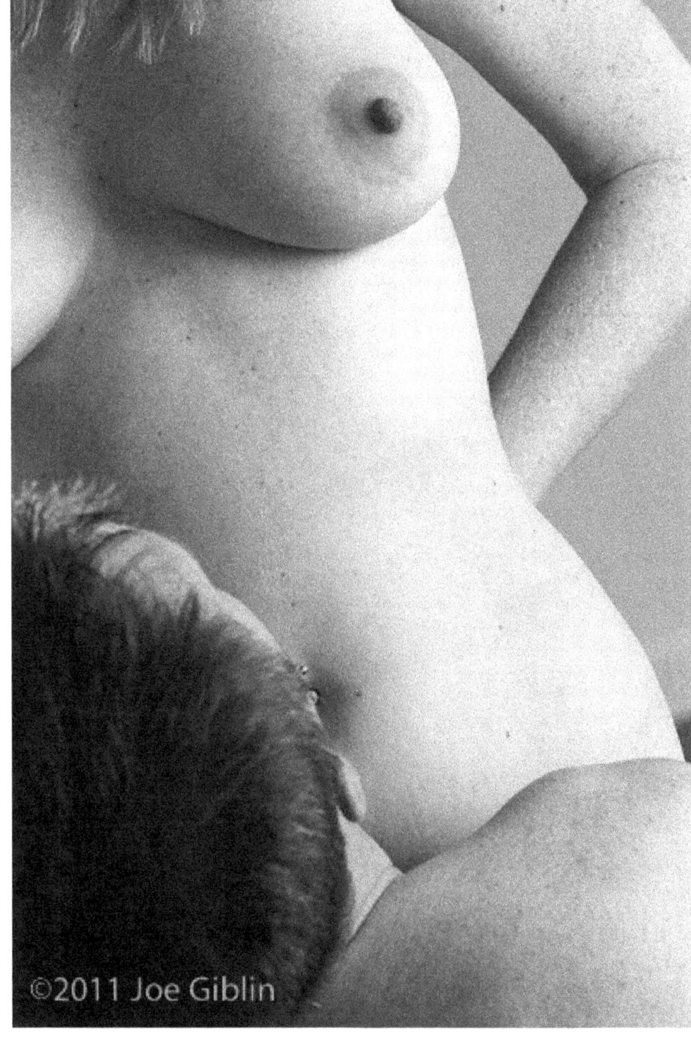

Joseph Giblin is a full-time freelance photographer that has shot erotic and fine art nude photos for over 20 years. His erotic images are represented in London by an online agency and can be seen on his website with a password. Visit www.joegiblin.com to see more.

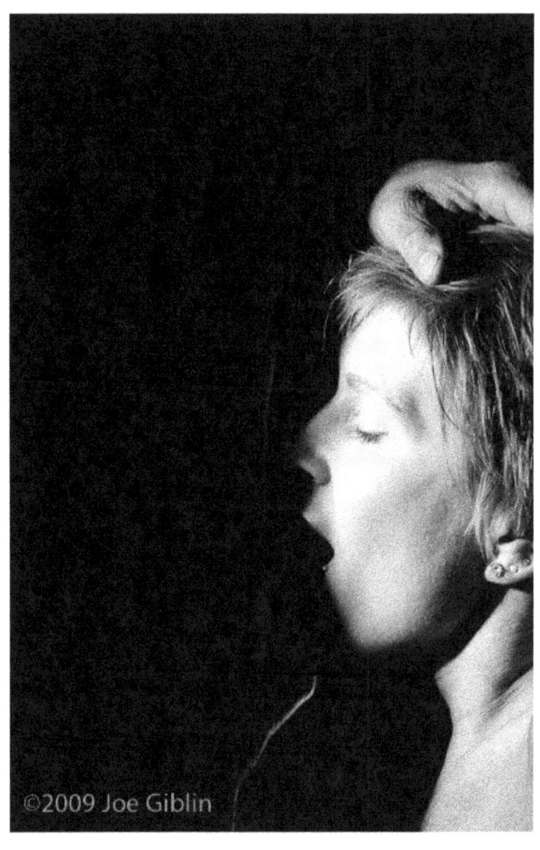
©2009 Joe Giblin

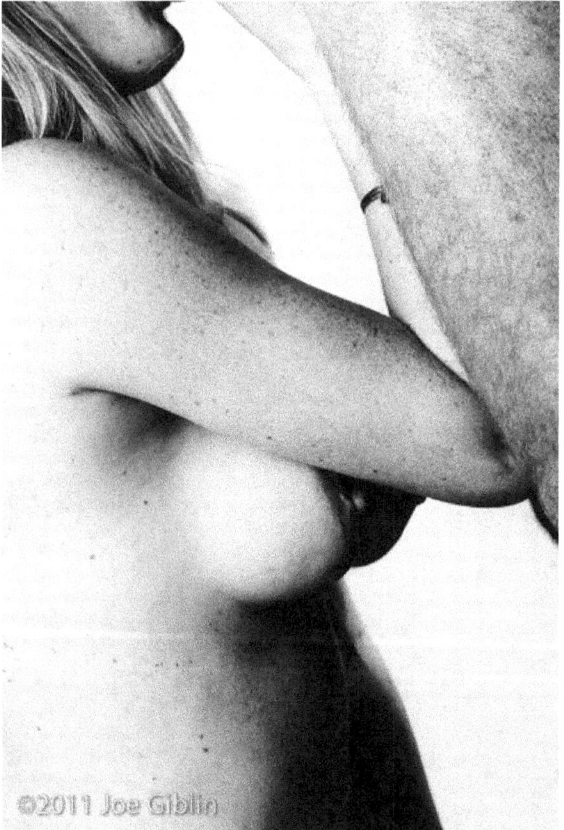
©2011 Joe Giblin

©2009 Joe Giblin

MY NIGHT WITH THE PRINCE

by Amanda Roberts

illustrations by Sophie Crow

I sat by the little pond behind the temple of Guanyin and breathed in the clean, crisp air. This was my favorite place to be in all of the Forbidden City. The sun was already setting, so it was cool and dark in the little grotto. The golden koi swam in circles below me, mistakenly thinking I was going to throw them some food. I could hear some frogs chirping, but could not see where they were hiding. I twisted a lock of my long, black hair in my fingers. I had such soft hair.

I turned when I heard some footsteps behind me. My eyes widened when the Emperor's brother, Prince Kong, wearing the yellow and golden robe I had embroidered for him, was standing there. I did my best to remain calm.

He smiled at me. "Evening, Suyi," he said.

I stood, straightened my skirt, walked over to him and *kowtowed* before him. "My Prince," I said with my face to the floor.

"Suyi!" he said, offering me his hand, "surely friends such as you and I are above such formalities."

I accepted his hand and stood. We left the little pool and walked down a long hallway decorated with teakwood carvings. "Are we ever above such formalities?" I asked. "Do not your wives and concubines still *kowtow* in your presence?"

He shrugged. "Some of the wives do; some do not. The concubines all do, though. My wives would beat them if they refused."

I rolled my eyes, shook my head, and smiled. "I was raised too poor to understand the intrigue of such large families," I said.

"The Empress paid for you with a very fine concubine to your father. How do you think your mother is handling her?" he asked.

My head instinctively dropped at the mention of my mother. "I don't know," I said. "My mother was very cold and hard. I am sure the poor concubine is miserable. Unless she has had many sons like the Empress promised. Maybe then my mother will be good to her."

He nodded. "Did you notice that I am wearing the robe you made for me, Suyi?"

I looked at him, from his neck to the floor. The robe was every bit as exquisite as I remembered. I had started with the finest yellow satin to make the shell of the robe. It was lined with the softest rabbit fur I could find. Then I used the most expensive golden thread to embroider the head of a massive dragon on the center of the back with its body, legs, and tail snaking out around the rest of the robe. I had embellished it with pearls all the way from the South China Sea. It was my magnum opus and had taken me two years to make.

My eyes wandered back up the robe and I looked at his face. On any other man, the robe might not have been as stunning, but on Prince Kong, with his broad build, strong jaw, long, black hair, and piercing grey eyes, he looked like a King.

He smiled at me as I surveyed him. He seemed to enjoy the fact that I was looking at him so intently. I finally managed to break my gaze away.

"You should stop praising me for that ugly robe," I said, turning from him and walking away. "It was a gift from the Empress, your dear brother's wife, as thanks for defending us against those invaders. It pains her for you to give me credit for her mighty gift."

"She did not make this robe," he said, catching up to me.

"She brought me from a dirt farm in faraway Hunan into her service. She provided the materials. She had the idea for the robe. Everything I am is because of her. Alone, I am nothing."

"Come into my household," he said, stepping in front of me causing me to stop and look up at him. "Some of my wives are skilled at embroidery, but with a fraction of your skill. I would be very pleased to have you under my roof. I would praise you and your skill publicly every day."

I scoffed. "You think I am just some weaver girl you can buy into your house? I am in service to Empress Cixi, the most powerful woman in the country. Only she deserves the best. You are only a Prince," I said waving my hand at him dismissively. I started to walk away from him, but he grabbed my arm and turned me back to him.

"Do you truly despise me, Suyi?" he asked.

"You are nothing," I said. "Just like me."

He pulled me close to him and kissed me. It was not the first time we had kissed, but this time is was different. Before, the kisses had been sweet, flirtatious, and I could easily run away. This time, there was something more firm, more insistent about his kiss. I could not have run away if I wanted to. There was a hunger to his kiss. He needed me.

He held one hand around my shoulders and the other around my waist. I reached up and put one arm around his neck. I wanted to comfort him, let him know that this time I wasn't going to run away. He tasted like pomegranates and felt so hot against me. I could hear a small growl escape his throat as he moved from my mouth to my neck where he began to bite and suck. I felt a throbbing and wetness between my legs. I had not lain with a man before, but I had felt desire and I knew that my body wanted him.

I gasped in surprised and jerked my hand back, but he held my hand tightly, almost too tightly as he kept staring into my eyes. He forced my hand to touch him. I did not shirk back this time and I let him show me what to do as I closed my hand around it and then gently stroked up and down.

He stopped kissing me and looked deep into my eyes. He took me led me down a dark hallways, away from any prying eyes. He put my hand inside his robe. He led me to his large, hard cock. I gasped in surprised and jerked my hand back, but he held my hand tightly, almost too tightly as he kept staring into my eyes. He forced my hand to touch him. I did not shirk back this time and I let him show me what to do as I closed my hand around it and then gently stroked up and down. He sighed, closed his eyes, and let go of my wrist. I kept moving my hand up and down. I could barely touch the tips of my fingers together, it was so thick and I was surprised when my fingers felt some soft hairs.

He wrapped his arms around me, burying me in the long sleeves of his robe. He placed his cheek next to mine and sighed as I continued pleasuring him. "Suyi," he whispered, "I want you to come to my room tonight."

I let go of his cock and took a step away. I looked up into his eyes, which were rimmed in red. "You think I am your slave to call when you want?" I asked.

"Never," he said. "I the most decorated Prince in all of China. I have wives and concubines for my pleasure. Any foolish maiden on the street would throw herself at my feet if I so desired."

I removed his arms from around my neck and stepped away. "I am no foolish maiden," I said.

He nodded. "Exactly," he said. "You are cold and utterly devoted to my dear sister-in-law. For you to choose to lay with me would be a great favor from you."

"It is more than a favor," I said. "Should we be caught, I could lose my life. I could be killed simply for daring to touch your great personage," I said glancing below his waist.

He stepped close again and kissed me gently. He squeezed one of my breasts with one hand and my backside with the other. "I am worth it," he whispered.

While I trembled and felt moist from his touch, his arrogance was appalling. I rolled my eyes and stepped away. "Not even you are worth a moment of my time, Prince Kong," I said. "Much less, my life."

I began to walk away, but he followed me. He grasped one of my arms and whispered in my ear, "Tonight, Suyi. Come to me tonight. I will dismiss my servants early and there will be no danger to you. Come to me."

I shrugged him off and kept walking. I did not look back at him. My heart was beating like a drum, my knees were weak, my stomach was dancing, but I managed to walk straight ahead until he was no longer behind me. I then ran to my quarters and looked at myself in the mirror. My face was flushed and my hands were shaking. My servant came to my side and asked if I was all right. I told her to mind her own business and to leave me for the rest of the evening. She did as she was told.

"I never said that," I finally said. "I only wanted to know what it was like to sleep like a princess for one night."

I poured water into my wash basin and rinsed my face. I could not believe what had just happened. Of course, I had felt a wanting for Prince Kong many times. He was so kind to me. He was the only person who openly acknowledged my embroidery skills. While my skills were known throughout the kingdom, Empress Cixi would only have the best in her service after all, humility was a cardinal virtue for a woman. I was never publicly praised and when the Empress thanked me in private, I kept my head low and denied the beauty of my work. But, secretly, I wanted to shout from the top of every temple in the empire that I was the greatest embroiderer. I wanted to return to my hometown and show my mother the Prince's robe so she could see how my talent had grown so far beyond hers. A thousand years from now I wanted people to sing laments about how no one ever created embroidery as beautiful as mine ever again. Prince Kong's public thanks for my work gave me a tiny glimpse into the glory I desired in my heart. And it made me desire him.

I knew I would never marry as long as I was in the Empress's service. I would never have children. My life was utterly devoted the Empress and I could not have such petty distractions in my life. Even taking a lover would mean less time working, more time worrying about my own wants or the wants of someone else. I could not afford such diversions to my work.

Then there was the very idea of lying with Prince Kong that was absurd. The royal family was above the rest of us, appointed and protected by the heaven. Only women, wives and concubines, appointed by the Emperor or Empress had the right to touch a man of the royal family. If I was caught, even my great skill and the love the Empress or the Prince had for me could not protect me.

I paced as all these thoughts ran through my head. Going to the Prince's room was an insane, deadly thought. All of my powers of reason told me not to do it. And yet, I wanted to go. As much as I hated it, I loved the Prince. It made me feel weak. Loving the Prince put me in danger and could only lead to disaster. I thought of my poor friend from childhood, Lily, who was banished from the embroidery school, sent home in disgrace for falling in love with the military boy and giving herself to him. Love had cost her everything.

Of course, Lily's weakness was also her carelessness. I caught her and in my stupid childhood innocence, betrayed her. I would not be so careless. In the darkness, after the servants were gone, I could give into my feelings, just this once. Being with him for just one night did not mean that I was his lover or that I was in love with him. One night of passion would not interfere with my duties to the Empress. But not giving into my feelings would interfere. I could think of nothing else. Even right now, I could be working but all I could think about was him. If I went to him, it would be over and he would no longer occupy my thoughts. I could return to my work clear of mind.

I waited until dark, and then I brushed perfumed oil through my hair, tied it up and decorated it with a string of jade beads. I put on my best purple robe and used a small amount of red color on my lips. I slipped out of my room and snaked my way through the grounds of the Forbidden City to the small palace he and his entourage were housed in. I waited at the end of the hall where the door to his room was until his guards passed out of sight. I crept to his door and tapped on it very quietly.

The door opened almost immediately, as if he were waiting for me. He smiled brightly, almost as bright as my yellow dragon robe he was still wearing, and his eyes shone. He grabbed my hand and pulled me inside. "Suyi!" he exclaimed. "I cannot believe you are here. As soon as you left my sight earlier, I thought I had made a terrible mistake. I was sure that you would never come to me."

"It is my goal to make sure you never know what I will do," I said.

"But you are here," he said stroking my face gently. "That must mean you do love me."

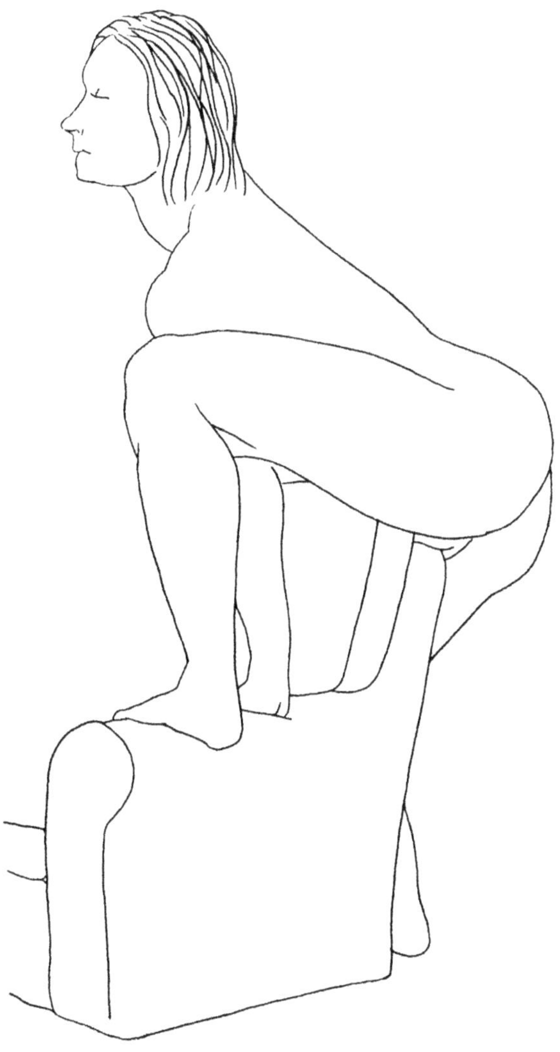

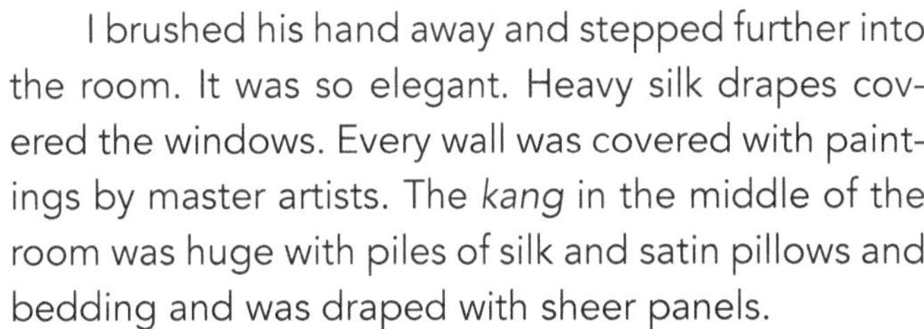

I brushed his hand away and stepped further into the room. It was so elegant. Heavy silk drapes covered the windows. Every wall was covered with paintings by master artists. The *kang* in the middle of the room was huge with piles of silk and satin pillows and bedding and was draped with sheer panels.

"I never said that," I finally said. "I only wanted to know what it was like to sleep like a princess for one night."

He looked me up and down as he walked over to me slowly. "Well you will only know that," he said as he undid the sash of my robe, "if you spend the night with a Prince."

He kissed me and took the pins and beads from my hair so it could flow freely. He kissed my cheek and my neck. He opened my robe and caressed my naked breasts. My nipples grew hard as he squeezed them. He was a head taller than me, so it was a little awkward as he bent to try and kiss my chest. I had never been naked in front of a man before, but he made me feel beautiful and confident. I didn't want to shrink away from him; I wanted him to touch every part of me. He stood back up and reached through my robe to grab my backside with both hands and pulled me to him as he returned to kissing my mouth. I could feel his hard cock poke me in the stomach as he did, which had the unfortunate effect of making me giggle like an idiot.

He stopped groping me and looked down at me confused. "My lovemaking humors you, my lady?" he asked.

I felt my face grow hot and I looked down to avoid his gaze. I wasn't sure what to say, so I undid the sash on his robe and opened it to reveal his naked body. It was fantastic. His imperial raiment concealed the body of a warrior. His chest was hard and every muscle was clearly etched on his skin. He had a scar on the left side of his stomach from a battle he had almost lost. His legs showed immense power form years of riding horses. His member, which had been fully erect and stabbing me only a moment ago, was now drooping a bit, dejected at my cruel giggles. I realized in that moment that he was in my power. His pleasure or his pain was at my bidding.

I ran my finger along his manhood and he took in a sharp breath. His head rolled back a bit and he sighed as he once again returned to attention.

"Tell me how to please you," I whispered.

He looked down and kissed me again before taking my hand and leading me over to the *kang*. He removed his robe and tossed it to one side. He slid his fingers over my shoulders and removed my robe as well. We stood naked before each other as equals. Both vulnerable, both full of desire. Just a man and a woman, not a prince and simple court artisan. He sat on the edge of the *kang* and motioned for me to sit in front of him. I got down on my knees, between his, and my face directly across from his cock.

"Touch it," he said.

I gently ran my fingers down one side, causing him to gasp again. He wrapped my fingers around him and showed me how to move my hand up and down, with my thumb hitting below the tip, just the way he liked it. He moaned quietly to my touch. I could feel myself growing wet knowing that I was pleasing him. Oh, how I wanted him to touch me in such intimate ways.

He reached down and ran his fingers through my hair then he pulled my face closer to his cock.

"Kiss," he said.

I was a bit surprised at first, and it seemed a little strange. I wanted to laugh to cover the fact that I felt uncomfortable, but I didn't want to hurt his feelings again, so I leaned in and gave a small kiss near his snake's eye. I looked up at him for approval. I wasn't sure how this little kiss could please him. He was smiling and ran his thumb over my lips.

"Open your mouth," he said. "And take me inside."

This seemed even stranger to me. I didn't know a lot about love making, but I didn't think his member was supposed to go into my mouth. I was aching between my legs and wanted him

I wanted to laugh to cover the fact that I felt uncomfortable, but I didn't want to hurt his feelings again, so I leaned in and gave a small kiss near his snake's eye. I looked up at him for approval.

to touch me there. He must have noticed the confusion and apprehension in my face. This time he chuckled.

"Don't be scared," he said. "Just try it for a minute."

I opened my mouth and he guided the head of his cock inside. He put his hand behind my head and moved me slightly forward and back so he went in and out of my mouth. He tasted salty, but he was certainly enjoying himself, moaning and panting, so I didn't stop. He gripped my hair as I tried to move my mouth and tongue all around his cock. He tried to force me to take him deeper, but I made a horrible gagging sound. He let go of my hair and stroked my cheeks.

"I'm sorry, Suyi," he said. "We will have to work on that next time." He looked at me with gentle eyes and I didn't have the heart to tell him that there wouldn't be a next time. He pulled me up towards him and laid with me on the *kang*. He kissed me and stroked my hair and face. He massaged my breasts and once again made them pique with interest. He began kissed down my throat and chest and then flicked one of my nipples with his tongue. His breath felt cool on the now wet nipple which made my body feel prickly all over. He sucked, kissed, and bit all over my breasts as he slowly moved on top of me.

This was how it was supposed to be, I thought. I wanted him on me, around me, inside me. I opened my legs when I felt his hand petting my soft hairs. I could feel him smile through his kisses as he touched my wetness.

"I'm glad you want me, Suyi," he whispered.

"I would not be here if I didn't, my Prince," I answered.

At that, he positioned himself between my legs and laid completely on top of me. I could feel his cock touching and prodding me, looking for its way in. His body was much bigger than mine, this battle-built stag trying to mount a small domesticated mare. I spread my legs as far as I could and arched my hips to welcome him into me. He finally found it and I could not help but moan as just the head of his cock entered my body. He pulled out and then entered me again. He repeated this motion several times over and I groaned every time he pulled out and gasped in pleasure every time he entered.

He then reached around with one arm behind my backside. He pulled out, and while I expected him to enter again gently, that is not what happened. He held me firmly and shoved the full length of his cock inside me. I gasped in horror as pain shot through my entire body. I am sure I screamed because he then placed a hand over my mouth, but my head was swimming in confusion, pleasure, and terror. I felt as though I had been run through with a sword.

Prince Kong kissed my cheek and shushed me. He rubbed my hips and said words to calm me. "My sweet Suyi. I'm sorry. I knew you were a virgin and it would hurt. I didn't want to scare you, so I did it quickly."

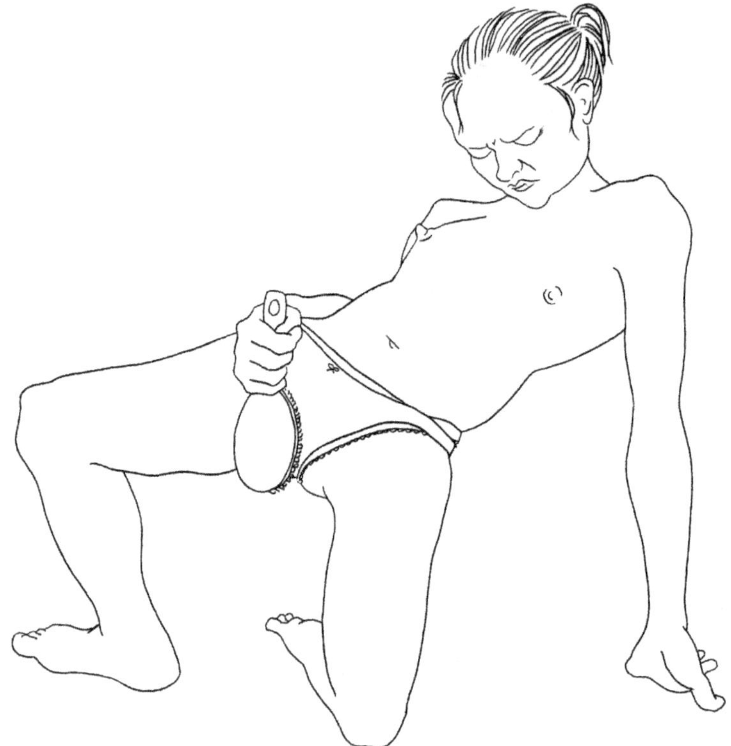

I was angry and sad at the same time. Part of me wanted to slap his face and stomp away. Another part of me wanted to curl up into a ball and cry. Was this it? Was this sex? This pain was something people killed, lived, and died for?

"Is…is that…it?" I finally managed to ask while choking back tears.

He kissed my face. "No, no, my dear. That was just the worst part since this is your first time. When you are ready, we can keep going."

I didn't know what he meant by 'keep going,' but I didn't want the one night I was going to spend with him to end like this, in pain and tears. I nodded and whispered, "keep going."

He nodded and slowly began to pull his full girth in and out of me. I was sore, but as he continued to make love to me, with sweet kisses, soft caresses, and skillfully entering and exiting my body, I calmed down and returned to the state of ecstasy I was in before.

Once he got into a steady rhythm, he gripped my shoulders, placed his cheek against mine, and panted with each thrust. I loved feeling his hot breath on my skin, his body form sweat under my fingers, and the way his cock now so easily slid in and out of me. Our bodies moved as one and I took great pleasure in the fact that he was enjoying my body as much as I was enjoying his.

I don't know that I ever climaxed, the entire experience felt so good and was so exhilarating that every moment was euphoric, but I do know that he did. With one last hard thrust and groan, he spilled into me, filling me with warmth and satisfaction.

Afterwards, I lay in his arms for a long time. I knew the sun would rise and I had to return to my room before anyone could catch me, but I didn't want my night with the Prince to end too soon. One night of selfish pleasure ad been too much to ask for and it couldn't happen again. So I savored him. I breathed his scent in deeply. I ran my fingers over every muscle and every scar on his body. I licked the salt from his cheek. This moment would have to last me a lifetime.

Amanda Roberts is an American writer who has been living and writing in China for over three years. She has recently starting writing erotica set in ancient China. Her first piece was published by Peaches Magazine *in the summer of 2013.*

Sophie Crow is an artist and illustrator living in Norwich, UK who is fascinated with all things to do with sexuality and the occult. Her latest project is WANK *an illustrated book about female masturbation, it takes 12 real life confessions found online of the inventive ways that woman masturbate and sensitively illustrates them.*

SEX POSITIVE: ACCEPTING IS FREEING

by Serena

My status as a classic porn star has made my life quite nice. I fucked a lot of people to get here, and am not ashamed of that. That was the job! I've traveled to places I'd never have gone, been put up in elegant hotels, and been treated with respect and admiration. I've been paid to be beautiful and to stir lust in the hearts of others.

Sexuality has been a part of my life since I was a tot; kids have an innate sense of their bodies. I consider my exhibitionism to be due to my manic bi-polar disorder. Through it I've learned to become "sex positive." It is something I've had to work on; I'm naturally a very jealous person. I've learned over my life that jealousy is a limiting emotion, though. "Sex Positive" is a state of mind I wish for everyone, it's an acceptance. Accepting is freeing. You needn't hold onto prejudices so tightly; you are

free to pursue your own brand of what's right for you. Holding onto anything too tightly makes you clenched, closed and constipated. Realize that there is no normal; there are attitudes as individual as you can be. There may be types of kinks, as there are types of animals, but humans tend to be even more different from one another. We come from a nurture/nature mix to create personalities. You are unique, no one has lived in your skin, so flaunt what makes you You!

Sex is the glue that binds a loving relationship or makes for a fun romp with strangers. Even when partaking of kinky sexual play, the more courteous you are to your partner out of bed the better the sex.

My own wish is that people have fun exploring their "dirty" sides, while hoping they never (really) hurt each other. Although I must say, a good spanking can wake you up! The red hot tingle on your butt cheeks will make you cry with pleasure!

If you are lucky enough to have a partner, love them. I hope the two (or more!) of you can be sexual playmates and let loose. Try things! You aren't being tested. No matter how absurd a request, realize the strength it took to ask. Always respond in a loving way. Try it! You might like it!

Sex was put here to make children and now that we can control that, sex can be FUN. Sex is here to stay, so make the most of your experience. Be brave, indulge yourself. Masturbation is a real asset to your day. Playing with yourself is very comforting. By masturbating you take the edge off; you are more relaxed. You can better show your lover what it is that truly gets you off. Masturbation can ward off loneliness. It can teach you to love yourself, literally. It is said you must love yourself first, before anyone else can. I have found that to be the physical truth.

To achieve orgasm is one of the highlights of life, a very precious thing; a moment deserving of rapture and passion is simply wonderful.

Savor time shared with your bedmate, too, as these are your most special times together. Sex is the glue that binds a loving relationship or makes for a fun romp with strangers. Even when partaking of kinky sexual play, the more courteous you are to your partner out of bed the better the sex. Make-up sex after fighting just isn't what it's cracked up to be. It's better to save your energy and not fight at all. You can get more favors if you ask with honey instead of sourness on your lips. "Be–Cum–One" is my motto. Frequency is not necessary. Quality of the act is what you want, moments you'll remember; sexuality that knocks you into sleep, into pleasant dreams.

Of course, the artists and writers have always known that Sex is a worthy subject, as they depict the nude human body and sexuality. In Chinese and Japanese art there are many silk screens painted with people fucking.

I worked on the movie sets, I considered my fuck scenes a service, an art, an example to my audience. I was a teacher, performing sex-ed. Fucking to me was close to sitting down to a fine meal, tasting of other›s desires, while satisfying my own. Granted, this overt, high sexual drive was due to my mental condition as well as youth. But being diagnosed bipolar still doesn't make me ashamed; I just see the hypocrisy more clearly in haters and finger-pointers.

People ask me what I want. I won't say "world peace" because that will never happen, at least until mankind leaves the planet. There are too many power hungry demagogues; too much greed, and not enough compassion. What I want is for people to be able to express their sexuality openly, without shame. I want for people, anyone, to marry whomever they want… gay and lesbian couples and couples of different races and religions. We are all people, and all people need love. Love comes in all shapes and sizes and colors. I want to be able to enjoy sex until old age; a very old age. Not just for me but for everyone.

Art by christopher Chamberlain

MY AFTERNOON NAP

by Serena

Whenever possible, I snatch some of the afternoon for myself. I set time aside just for masturbation. I want to be pleasured, and I am alone. I guide my hands over my body, exploring the places that hide beneath my clothes. I love the quiet, yet yearn to be stimulated. I will enjoy the solitude of my beautiful room, and feel free to send screams out the windows. The neighbors aren't close.

Dancing into the other room, I check out my body in the full length mirror. My legs are strong and push my pelvis up to the mirror's view. I want to see my puss, and reach down to touch my toes, looking in the mirror. Stuck in the air like this, I think of you coming by, catching me with pussy in the air. I'm ready for you, willing to be had. Oh! I can feel your strong hands on my ass cheeks, pulling my butt apart, massaging it and then -- SLAP! Ouch! I know my cheeks are bright red, I feel the sting. "Oh," I groan. I am ready for you to have your way with me, but remember that you are just my imagination!

The drill noise of my vibrator sounds as if we're adding on an addition to our sweet little house. If you were a spy, you'd peek at me doing things to my breasts and ass that I alone do to my body.

So my new plan is a date with my vibrator upstairs, at least until you arrive home from work.

The drill noise of my vibrator sounds as if we're adding on an addition to our sweet little house. If you were a spy, you'd peek at me doing things to my breasts and ass that I alone do to my body. Enjoying the moisturizer, I spread lotion all over. My entire body gets a rub. I spank my thighs and I laugh! I thrust out my butt to see its curves.

Off go my slippers and jeans as I throw myself into bed. As I dive in I grab a butt plug and the lube. I use a finger to guide the plug in, grab my vibrator to ease the pain of getting fucked in the ass. My hand pushes hard, my clit getting big and sore. My ass swallows the plug whole and I use the vibrating end of my wand to ease the pain of my clit button about to explode in pain.

I sit on my ass, holding the plug in place. Pain and pleasure turn to desperate wanting. Stroking the shaft of my wand like a long prick, jerking it off, I stick my clit up to meet its moving part, my ass still filled. My clit is really starting to go crazy. My dick is my "magic wand" and I am stoking it. It is so hard; I push the wand onto my clit, my aching clit. My clit needs release. I sit flatter on my ass, pushing in the butt plug further. My clit is being rubbed raw it seems, and I groan from deep within. "Oh, I'm gonna cum."

I can't take much more. I lose all thought except the need of my clit. I close my eyes and my hips begin to rock. The lightening strike of orgasm hits me behind the eyelids and my crotch seems to pour out pussy fluid. The surge of pleasure comes from my belly up through my throat and out comes a savage howl! I fall on my vibrator, on the pillows and the mattress. I push the wand away and keep falling; falling into a deep afternoon sleep, waking when the plug slips out from my ass.

Serena has starred in over 110 adult films, has appeared in magazines such as Hustler *and* Playboy, *and is an inductee of the X-Rated Critics Organization Hall of Fame as a film pioneer. He new biography is being published by BearManor Media and will be out suring the summer of 2014.*

POND WATER

photos by Jeffrey Fletcher

ARTIST STATEMENT:

The work you are viewing here is a collection of images I've produced as part of an investigation into the possibilities of adapting surrealist techniques of automatism to photography as a tool to investigate the relationship between erotics and aesthetics. The concern is with both the external and internal image, how they are formed, how they interact and what influence they have on us.

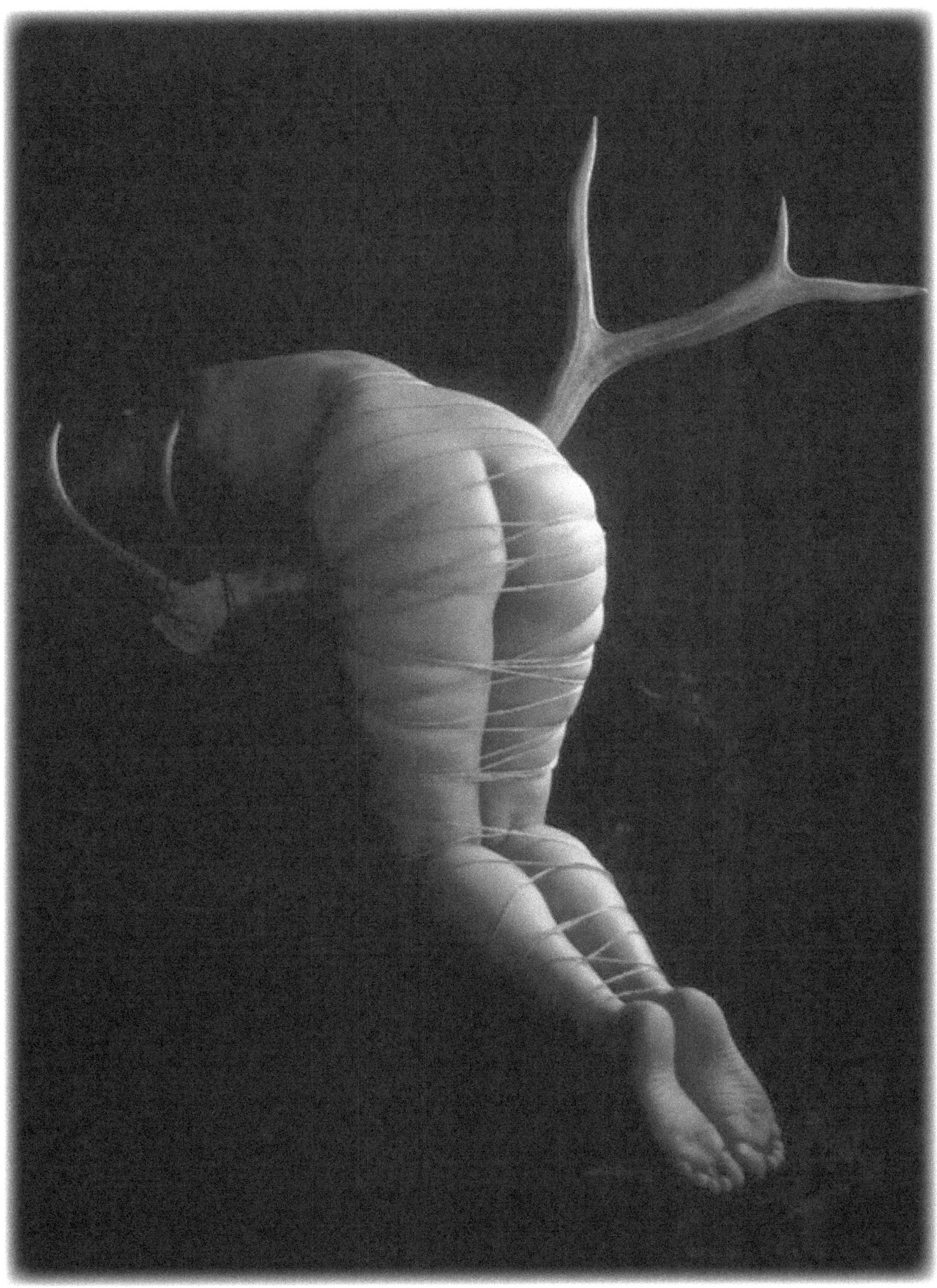

To produce the work film is often run through the camera several times, sometimes it's soaked in pond water until the emulsion starts to decay. The slides are then scanned and moved into a digital environment where some work is done to clean them up and develop the aesthetic potential of the images.

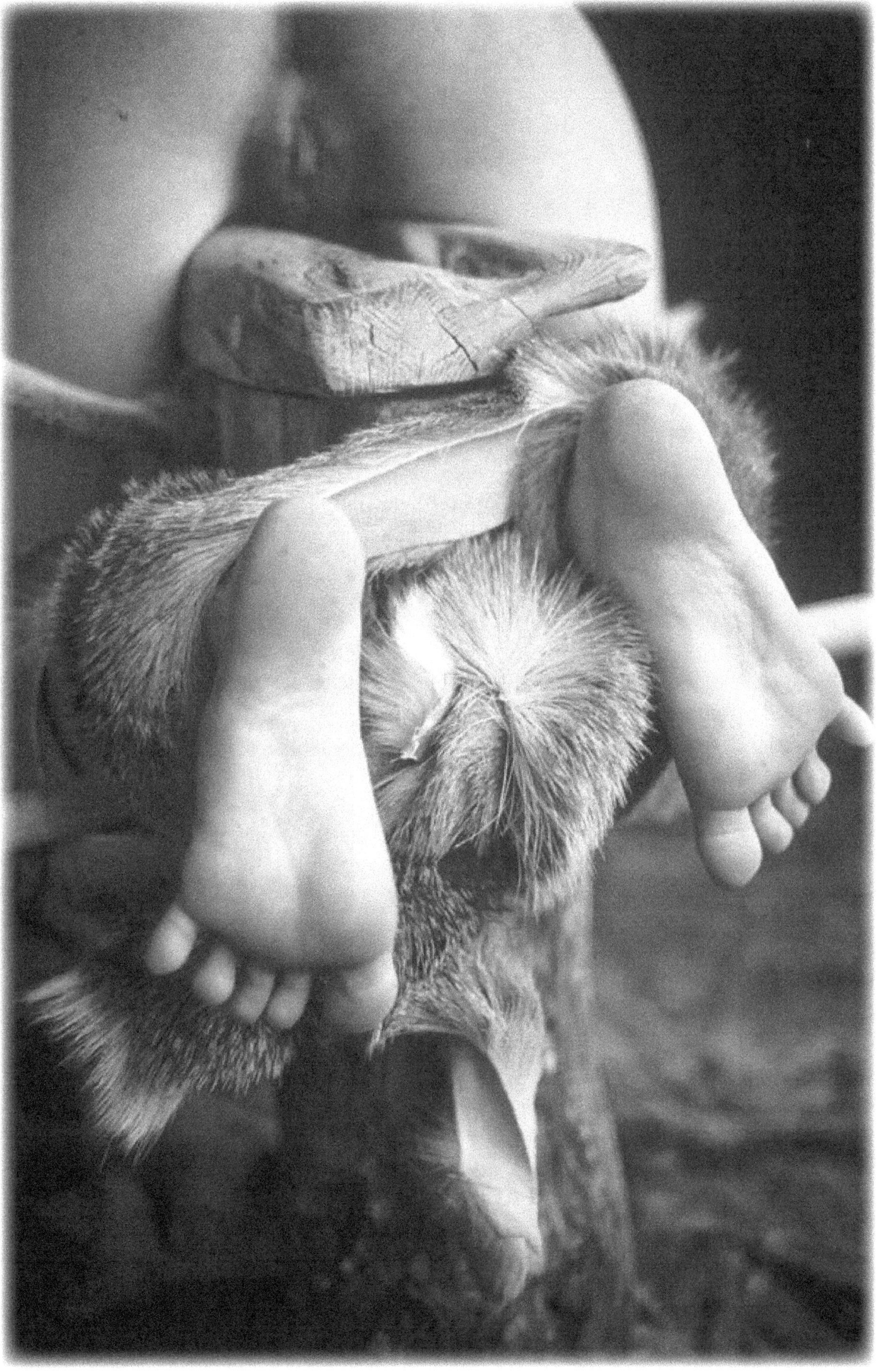

ONE DAY NAKED

by The Mrs.

photos by Nate Edwards

It was Thursday. I got up. I thought, today, I'm not wearing any clothes. That was it. No thinking about it the day before.

No impressive dreams of walking Idaho as I slept. There wasn't anything deep about it.

I was not a nudist. I worked at Ameris, a family-type bank, whatever that means, across from Popeye's Chicken and an indie drug store and I wore clothes every day of my life.

Probably, I'd just snapped. But when I came out of the shower that morning, after putting on my underarm Ban, I looked at my shirt, laying there on the washing machine, and I just decided.

Right now felt right.

The shirt. It wasn't for me.

I got ready, as usual, just without the clothes. It took me a lot less time. Though it still took my hair the same amount of time to dry. I let the air dry the rest of it. I had to hang onto my house keys, since I had nowhere to put them.

No one stopped me. Everyone looked, and laughed, after I passed them. But no one stopped me.

I got on the bus without a problem because the driver didn't notice, and only a couple ladies over 50 cared. Everyone else ignored me. I crossed my legs. My man-purse concealed a few things. I'd decided to bring it. I had to have somewhere to keep my lunch money. Does this mean I wasn't 100% nude? Who was going to add the percentages together anyway?

Once I got to the office, I just put it on the desk. The man-purse. Not that I was hiding behind it. I switched on the computer and checked the market. My job was analyzing how the bank could reinvest the limited capital it had borrowed from patrons at 1%. Money markets were down to .05% now. CDs were what MMs were 6 years ago. The economy was terrible.

"Jason wants – what the hell are you doing?!"

Of course I was doing anything when Amelia had popped her young permed head in. I always kept the door open.

"What happened? Were you mugged?" and she started to giggle.

> **"You," Jason told him, "get this man a towel, prefer-ably get him any clothes and – "**
>
> **"I won't wear them," I said.**
>
> **"What? Why not?"**
>
> **"I'll just take them off again."**

I smiled at her. "Jason wants to see me?"

"Not this much!"

I laughed, and started to slap her back in appreciation, but she just ran out, her loose white shirt billowing in the cool air conditioning.

I made my way to the deputy manager's office. There was the sound of spilling papers, coffee, screams behind me. Well, from my angle everything felt wonderful. Like a waterless shower.

Knocking, hearing the "yeah," I stuck my head in and said, "What's up?"

"We've got someone coming from regional around one," Jason said. "After lunch anyway. If you can collect up last quarter's – what are you wearing?"

"Nothing."

He waited. Then said, "Nothing?"

"Last quarter's summations or all the guesswork?"

"Why are you so naked?"

I shrugged. Let's face it, I lot of shoulder this time. It was difficult to answer why. Plus, he always kept the A/C on extra in his office and it was getting me hard.

"Are you okay?" he asked. His face was going red.

"Oh, yeah. Don't worry – "

"Get some clothes on! Now!"

"Well…"

"*What*?"

"I'd rather not. If it's all the same."

He would've done that boss thing of coming closer, taking his glasses off, I could guess, but he wasn't coming forward at all.

"It's not all the same. What's the *matter* with you?

I laughed, a little.

"Take the day off," he said.

"No, I'm fine."

"No, I'm *telling* you to take the fucking day off. And if you *ever* come in here like this again… Geez. You didn't walk through the lobby…"

He got back behind his big Arminian desk and dialed something short. Just seconds passed and Griffith came in. He was a short, wide guy, an ex-golfer, used to being bored all day. So standing just inside the entrance in a uniform that didn't look quite right was the perfect retirement job for him.

He about had a giggle fit when he saw me. Funny how many people didn't see me. "I wondered where you got to. Damn, Tommy."

"Hey," I said back coolly. "Don't mock it 'til you try it."

"You," Jason told him, "get this man a towel, preferably get him any clothes and – "

"I won't wear them," I said.

"What? Why not?"

"I'll just take them off again."

Griffith thought while Jason bubbled, trying not to look, but looking. "We need you a straight jacket then."

"Tommy, what are you saying?"

"I'm sorry," I told Jason. "I've never felt more free."

"Oh god."

"I never even thought about it before. You know. You get the sudden urge. I could die like this."

"Are you serious?" and Jason just kept his mouth open after that.

"Yeah."

"*Why?*"

"Let's call the cops," Griffith said. I always expected him a closet homophobe.

"No!" Jason shouted. "There's nothing wrong here. Tommy. I need you to do this. For me."

"Oh, I know."

"Get some *clothes* on!"

"I'm fine."

Griffith started to move. Why, I don't know. He wasn't obviously going to land hands on me.

"Do you want to get fired?"

"Of course not!"

Jason was ready to tear his hair out. It was my coolness, I guess. "How did you *get* here?"

I started to tell him about the bus and how the seats feel when it's just you on them, trying to convince him like only the newly converted can. The feeling of vibration on your balls going up and down. How you can *feel*, finally, the road again. The lovely road. The sensation of – *everything*. Rebirth. There's not much like it. But by the time I'd come out of my descriptive fever, Jason was dialing 911 and Griffith stood between me and the door until the ambulance arrived. I tried to restate my sensations. That it was nothing sexual, just – liberating. It's really no different than taking your coat off in a warm room. Well, those guys both wore ties, the most unnecessary of clothes, so there was no common ground here.

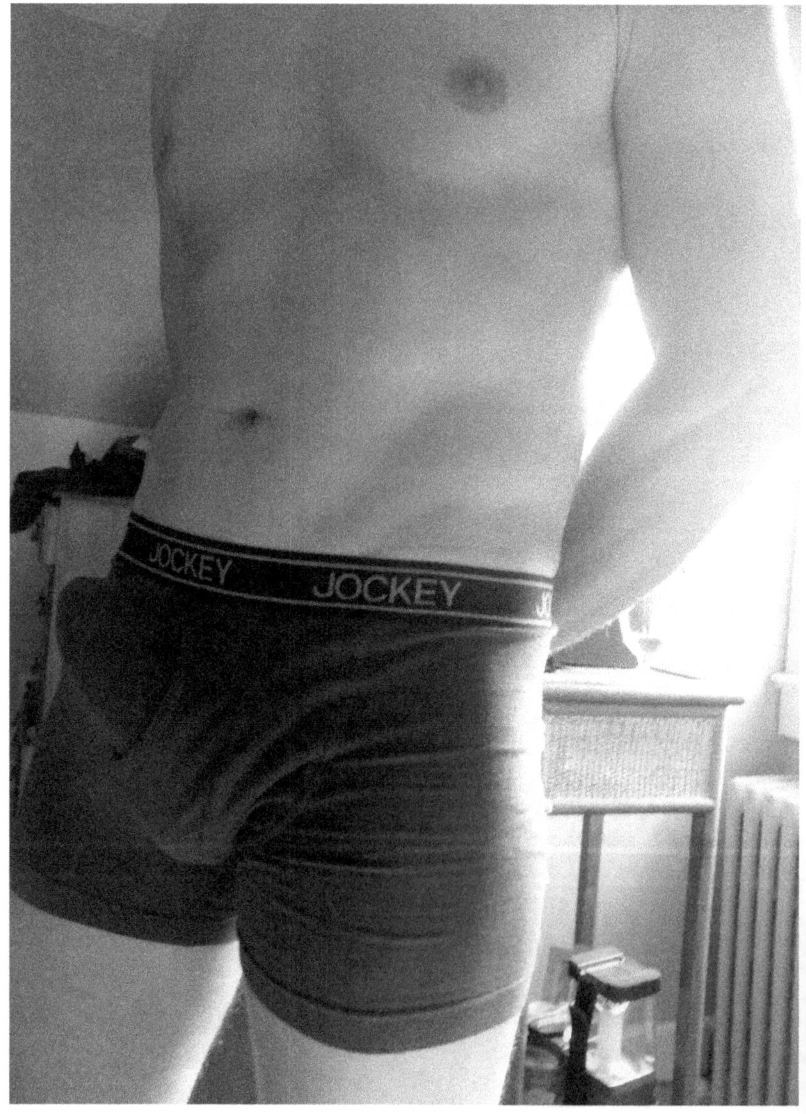

It only took a few minutes for the ambulance to arrive. We were near the campus (University of Idaho) and they had a student-run teaching hospital. How the paramedics were both over 40, I don't know. They strapped me into a mobile

One of the guys ran in and came walking back with a thin young cop who smiled at me. The meds undid me and the cop put me in cuffs and walked me inside. They let me keep the sheet, but I kept trying to get out of it.

bed, wrapped me up tight in a white sheet with straps along the edges. Once we got in the ambulance no one was sure what to do since I wasn't in pain at all. Until a few minutes ago, I felt great.

"Where are your clothes?" one med asked.

"At home."

The other unbuckled me, once the door was closed, took the sheet off, and started feeling me up. Massaging up my leg, I guess, watching my face, until his hand was on my dick. I'm afraid I was up. Well, it was still the morning, you know, and all this was new.

Either he wasn't a perv or I wasn't his type. The other guy took my blood pressure, temperature, did the light in my eyes. The non-perv knocked on the wall and made a sign to the driver through the little door, then came back to strap me in again.

"Do you know where you are?"

"Where?"

"Do *you* know?"

"In an ambulance?" I asked.

The meds nodded to each other and soon we pulled up at Whitney Police Station on the Five Points side of town. Then I realized Jason must have called the medics not the cops so it would seem like a health thing and they'd wrap me. No one comes around Five Points if they can help it. Nothing to do with crime. There's just nothing here.

One of the guys ran in and came walking back with a thin young cop who smiled at me. The meds undid me and the cop put me in cuffs and walked me inside. They let me keep the sheet, but I kept trying to get out of it.

Even when the cop sat me down in the large room full of desks, I kept unrolling the sheet, trying to get the knots out of the straps around my arms, until he gave up and just spent his energy trying to find keys on the computer.

"Name."

"Tom Brown."

"Is that your real name?"

"Are you going to take my fingerprints?"

"Oh yes."

"Tommy Wallace. But I was born Danny R. Wallace."

"Address."

This kept up for 15 minutes. I asked to see an attorney, but after they took my fingerprints, they put me in a holding cell with six other guys. I didn't have the sheet. In case I hanged myself? The place stank.

Now, being in a cell, naked, with other men wasn't what I thought it would be. It was very heterosexual. I'm very hetero. I subscribe to private.com and hustler.com and wifeysworld.com. But I was still kind of disappointed that no one touched me. No one even looked at me all the minutes I was there. I wasn't *repulsive*. I had a paunch, but –

"Wallace!"

I was taken – someone put a big blue denim jacket around me – to a small room and I waited, alone, naked (they took the jacket back), until a young woman entered. She was slight and brown-haired and enjoyed her light brown suit, you could tell. I guess no one told her anything because she was very surprised. I told myself she was impressed by my dong size, because she sat and she tried not to look at it, tried not to smile and I thought of scratching and resisted with every fiber.

"Tommy? My name is Jackie. Can I ask why you're nude?"

"It felt right today."

"What felt right?"

"Not having anything next to my skin."

"Is that a problem for you? Usually?"

"Not usually. Don't you ever want to do that? Just, don't you ever feel like just chucking off all your clothes and going out as nature intended you?"

"Nature never intended for me to be this fat."

She wasn't fat. But she had kind of a round face. And her eyebrows were too far up on her head.

"You don't *have* to eat Pringles," I said.

"It's Long John Silver, actually. There's one on my corner, for God's sake!"

"Oh no."

"Yeah."

"Well."

She nodded. We both knew it wasn't her fault there was a Long John's there.

She was looking in a file that only had a single sheet of paper in it. "According to your record, you have no record." She scooted the file down the table. "So. Tell me. Have you had any shocks of late? Something that, without knowing it, could contribute..."

I thought about that. "My girlfriend killed herself four days ago."

"Oh God..."

"I didn't really like her." I shrugged. "She liked doing puzzles. We didn't have much in common. She had short hair."

"How long had you been going out?"

"Mostly she came over, and we had sex and did puzzles."

"Were you in love?"

"What do you mean? In love *with* her?"

"Take your time," she whispered.

"She started doing puzzles at the same time as doing me. I yelled at her."

"And... you think it was your... you feel responsible?"

I didn't get her for a while. "Oh. No. That was days ago. You

It was funny, being the only blatantly nude man in there. I could tell men's arms were working and they were trying to disguise their "shame." What was funny was the fact that only here was I being watched.

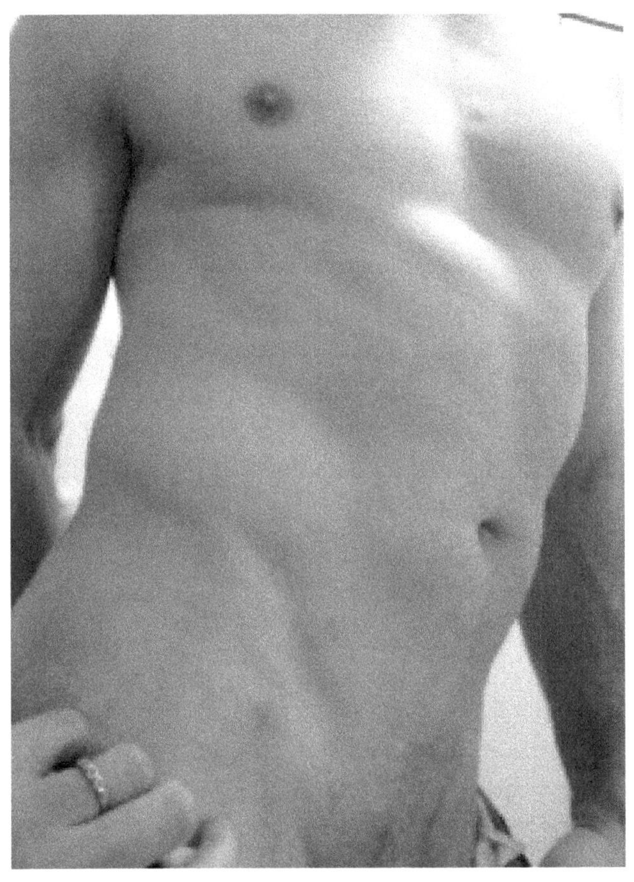

get used to things."

"You got used to the puzzles."

"We did it from behind so she could still do the puzzles…"

"Yeah. I'm sorry."

"I guess the worst thing was," I said, trying to get the emotion out of my voice, "when she finished, she just crumbled them back in the box. I wouldn't've minded if she hung them. Hung them like art. If she was proud of them. In a frame."

"You thought she was wasting her time."

"And my time!"

She looked at me, not my dick, for a change. "What do you want to happen now?"

"What do you mean?"

"Well, the bank's not going to press charges. They want you to have some rest. If it's without pay, if you get to come back, that's between you and your employer. My question is – if we let you go, fully clothed, are you going to be good?"

"Good, or nude?"

She looked at with sideway eyes. "You don't know the difference?"

"Can I make a phone call?"

Jackie gave me her cell and asked if I wanted privacy, but I just called and I asked Maggie, the girl in the apartment below me, to use my key on the windowsill (the key was painted white, sitting on the white sill, so it was hidden) and get me some clothes. She hardly knew me, didn't know why I was calling *her*, but she did it. I was out of there less than two hours later.

I was standing there, at the bottom of the stairs of the 12th Precinct, taking off the clothes she'd brought. I was smiling at her, saying, "I really appreciate all this."

"What are you doing?"

I tried to fold them for her. When I was naked and could breathe again, Maggie was gone. Grossed out. I looked pretty good. I was free.

I walked and walked. I was maybe four blocks from the station before the screaming began. Then people rushed, and I heard sirens. I ran, with everything swinging, and bought a ticket to see *Teacher's Pet 14* at The Gigglian, the retro porn theatre converted from the old Home Depot on Sasaya Street. I had my wallet in my hand. I guess Jason had sent it along from my bag at the bank.

It was funny, being the only blatantly nude man in there. I could tell men's arms were working and they were trying to disguise their "shame." What was funny was the fact that only *here* was I being watched. A couple of the dirty old men brigade, in their long, unnecessary coats, came closer, seat by seat. I did likewise, moving away. I wanted to see how *14* ended, and if it didn't end, how did it set up for *15*. Well, there was just a cum shot and that was it.

By the time the feature ended, the streets were clearer. The moon was beaming more visibly. It was growing cooler, more comfortable.

I walked toward the center of town. Mouths came open. Boys and women guffawed. Some teacher looking dude maybe yelled as I passed. Someone splashed me with something sticky from above. Mt. Dew maybe.

"Hey! Big Dick!"

It wasn't big, but I appreciated the kind words from whoever it was.

I went into a place I'd never been in. A large, mushroom-shaped building called The McCremery. It had an orange roof and was colder in here. My body was hot, believe it or not, and I chased everyone out just by being there. I gave the 40-year-old gal behind the ice cream tubs a smile of commiseration and ordered a double scoop of choco-walnut to make up for it, though it cost too much.

I just walked the street, not really wanting to go home, not caring about anything much at all now. Everyone continued to shout and scream and I was feeling insulted. One little girl ran up and slapped my dick and then ran away.

I mean, what's the point of that?

The breeze was great. It was the first time in my life that I'd *felt* it. Really understood what wind *is*. Like it was supposed to be felt. My feet hurt. That was the only drawback. I couldn't imagine going into a Goodwill shop, buying and wearing socks or flip flops. That wouldn't be betraying myself. I wasn't even an idealist, but I just couldn't imagine how that would look.

I walked and walked until I was beyond tired. Sleepy. The night man at Motel 6 refused to talk to me through the little plastic window and the Marriott on the corner opposite pledged to call the police within seconds. I wouldn't be coming back to either.

Well, there was a Motel Book within a few minutes walk, so I rubbed my arms and surprised myself by how cold my skin was. A car pulled up and a tall man in a suit rolled down the passenger window. The car needed a wash, but the man had a wily smile, and, like I said, I might be crazy, so I stopped when he stuck his head out a little and commenced small talk.

"How far you going?"

"Looking for a bed," I said.

"I sleep in one every night."

"I don't really go that way, sorry."

"What way you going?"

"I'm not gay," I explained.

"Oh!" It was like the thought had never occurred to him. Realistically hadn't. "I thought you looked lost. That's all."

Thinking a moment, all I could say was, "You've got a nice car."

"How far have you walked? You must be cold."

So I got in and he turned the heat up all the way, feet and main vents, and tried to drive while looking at me and telling me that he hadn't had the heat on since Winter and I said it's only Spring and he asked me if I'd like to drive.

"Why?"

"I could suck your cock while you drive."

"I told you, I'm not gay."

"Oh! Well. We don't *have* to be."

I thought this over. I really did love the feminine form. I was always punching the balls off myself when watching the Weather Channel ladies or interviews with Giada De Laurentiis or regular girls on whatboyswants.com.

"Who's going to know?"

I got behind the wheel, but I was a little nervous having no license and no clothes and really feeling the grainy rawhide urethane seat cover digging into my butt hair. Well, when he leaned over with his mouth open and I saw him in the dim dial light for the first time and how ugly he was, I just put a hand on his vague crown of golden hair and said no.

"Who's going to know?"

"God," I said. That seemed to put a cap on it. He fumed all the way to his place.

My naked foot often fell off the accelerator, but I got us there. I guess he invited me up to his couch just in case something would happen. I was *sleepy*.

"I'm really not too gay," I explained.

"Come on," he insisted. "You must be cold."

"I better not."

"Why?"

"I'm not looking for..."

"What? What are you not looking for?"

"I don't know," I had to admit.

I bid him goodbye and took to the road. Really the sidewalk. Which hurt; all the grainy glass and whatever you don't expect. And my dick was hard.

A dog started following me. I stopped to pet it, but his or her forehead between its eyes was wet so I didn't. He or she licked my balls anyway. It felt good.

I slept in a doorway. In fits. One time I woke up, thirsty, and there was a big red mark, like a clown's mouth, around the neck of my dick. When the sun came up, I had black ants in my crack. Maybe in my head hair, too. It itched!

The sun was beautiful. It set upon fluffy flat clouds. Then rose above them, like it was better than them. It was the first time in this God-forsaken Idaho that I'd actually seen it rise. I didn't even know it came up that far.

I walked. The only people up were old people and they scoffed and derided with little tongue sounds and talking louder to themselves than they otherwise would have. One teenager flicked my dick when I passed him getting on the bus. I preferred the old people.

I went into a place I'd never been in. A large, mushroom-shaped building called The McCremery. It had an orange roof and was colder in here. My body was hot, believe it or not, and I chased everyone out just by being there. I gave the 40-year-old gal behind the ice cream tubs a smile of commiseration and ordered a double scoop of choco-walnut to make up for it, though it cost too much.

I was too early for anyone at Ameris. Only the black crew that swept and polished and sat around drinking coffee in McDonald's paper cups were in there. They had the blinds down, but I could see inside. I guess someone must have called someone and I guess I had been standing there longer than I'd intended.

Jason hadn't had his shower yet. He had bad bed hair, I saw when he straddled out of his big Ford, and his brain looked fuzzy. He kept opening and closing his eyes like rebooting would help.

"Oh, Tom. What?"

"What?"

"You're still naked."

"I'm *cold*."

"And you've got ants." He picked one out of my armpit. A red one.

"Thanks."

"Are you ready to be sensible?"

"I'm sensible!"

"And a suit?"

I was. Actually, I was. The novelty was gone. "I'm just cold."

"Good."

"Can you drive me home? I'll suit up. You – "

"Well..."

"What?"

He looked at the sidewalk in a minute. "...They let you go..."

And I thought: isn't that life? Isn't that just how things are?

TOPLESS TOURISM

Photos by Lilah Rose

THE DECLARATION OF
INDEPENDENCE GROVE

JANSPORT

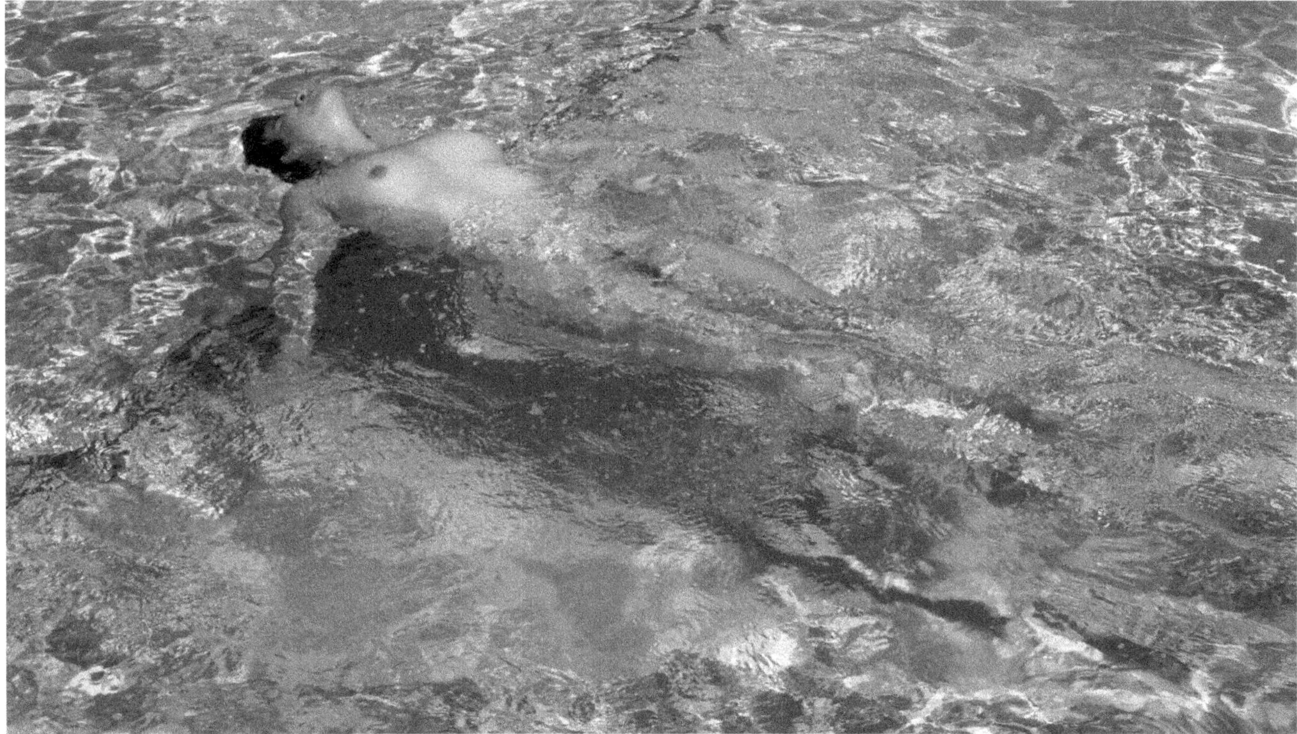

Lilah Rose is an artist, adventurer, and a keen equestrian. She has nimble fingers and never ceases to surprise.

ANOTHER NIGHT at the CUCK & BULL

by Vanessa Smythe

"Richard's taking me to the club tonight," his wife had said that morning, as he lifted a spoonful of cereal from the bowl. His eyes met her cool gaze as she took a bite out of her toast, her full lips pulled back from those big white teeth. He felt mixed feelings somewhere in the middle of his body: a stirring of arousal and apprehension both. All day at work, trying to focus on the numbers, he felt himself distracted.

Now Richard's arrival was less than an hour away. Susan, his wife, was bathing in preparation. He came into the bathroom, which was, in the style of modern suburban houses, large enough to house a small family, and there was Susan soaking in the oversized tub, two candles casting a radiant glow on her luscious pink skin. A breast surfaced above the waterline as she raised an arm to soap the join of limb and torso. As her husband entered, she exhaled softly, then pulled the plug. "Be a darling and hand me the towel," she purred. "I'd better get a move on, he'll be here soon," she said, padding her lithe body, toned by her regular pilate sessions, with the thick white towel. Making a show of looking for something he could not find in the bathroom cabinets, he watched in the mirror as she trimmed the little tuft of hair between her legs. Next she applied deodorant beneath her arms and expensive perfume, reserved for special occasions, to her body. This was always how she prepared.

"That smells sexy," he said.

"Mmm," she said distractedly, as she unwrapped a new pair of black thigh-highs and unrolled them onto her long slender legs, until they stopped a couple of inches from that neatly trimmed tuft of brown hair. The tuft soon disappeared beneath a small pair of black lace panties. "Which do you think?" she asked, holding up two pairs of earrings. "The pearls or the silver?"

"The pearls make you look more, well, respectable," he said hopefully.

He lingered, watching the completion of her outfit: a blouse cut to suggest the form of her breasts and allow a translucent glimpse of the black bra beneath; a short black skirt that hugged her hips; the bracelet around the right ankle; the black heels

He lingered, watching the completion of her outfit: a blouse cut to suggest the form of her breasts and allow a translucent glimpse of the black bra beneath; a short black skirt that hugged her hips...

and, finally, the silver earrings. She stood straight, brushed her hands down her body in a smoothing gesture, and smiled confidently at him. At just that moment the door bell rang.

Her heels clattered on the stairs as she made for the door. He was a few feet behind. He held back awkwardly as she pulled the door open. There stood Richard, all six feet two inches of man topped with a gleaming bald head. "You look great" he said, smiling broadly and holding out a bouquet of flowers to Susan. He looked sharp in a dark jacket that spread snugly across his broad shoulders and a maroon shirt that complemented his chocolate skin. Susan took the flowers then, holding them to the side, moved her body against his, putting her other arm loosely around his back, and planted her lips on his. They held the embrace for a good five seconds. The front door was still open and Susan's husband wondered anxiously if any neighbors could see this tall, dark man kissing his wife at the threshold of his home.

A few minutes later, after he and Richard spent a few moments exchanging pleasantries while Susan installed the flowers in a vase, he was climbing into the backseat of Richard's BMW. He pulled the seat belt across his chest. Richard and his wife sat in the front, and he felt oddly safe sitting in the back like a child watching his parents in the front seats. As Richard and Susan chattered idly above the hum of the engine, at one point he noticed Richard's hand move from the gear stick to his wife's thigh, slipping beneath the hem of her skirt to caress what lay beneath. Strapped in behind the driver's seat, he thought he saw his wife open her legs ever so slightly and flash a silent smile at Richard.

The BMW pulled into a dimly lit parking lot next to a nondescript boxlike building that had once served some industrial purpose but now pulsed faintly with the beat of electronica. There were already several cars parked there. They ranged from a gleaming Jaguar to a weathered old pickup, with a bumper sticker that said how much, forced to choose between fishing and his wife, the owner would miss his wife. The three of them emerged from the BMW. The car beeped discreetly as Richard clicked "lock" on his remote control, and Richard and Susan strode across the parking lot with Alan, her husband, at their side.

At the door they paused as Alan paid the cover charge for all three of them. Then they entered the discreetly lit space, about the size of a church hall, that housed the bar and dance area for the Cuck and Bull. To one side was the bar. A couple of dozen sets of tables and chairs stretched the length of one wall. The dance space, complete with a gleaming silver stripper pole (which Alan had always found tacky), was empty at this early hour. But little clumps of newly arrived patrons clustered by the bar and along the walls. The music was quiet enough to allow conversation, but the constant thrumming, just quicker than a normal heartbeat, was helping create a sense of mounting, expectant arousal among the drinkers.

Richard bought a cosmopolitan for Susan, a vodka and tonic for himself, and a ginger ale for Alan. As he was waiting for his drink, Alan looked around. You could tell the bulls from the husbands. The bulls, especially the wannabees who had shown up alone in search of a conquest, were more smartly dressed; with their brightly colored shirts and polished shoes, they reminded him of peacocks fanning their tails. Although none of the husbands were black, about a third of the bulls were. They knew that popular myths about black men hung like horses and the curiosity of suburban white women might help them to score tonight.

Many of the husbands, with no-one to conquer, looked as if they had set out for their neighborhood bar and wandered in here instead, by accident. Some wore ill-fitting jeans and nondescript shirts, as if they were trying not to draw attention to themselves: "my wife may be here in a short tight skirt with another man, but I'm not here with them; I'm dressed for another evening in front of the TV."

Some husbands stood at the bar with their wives, casting a wary eye at the men who approached with their pickup lines. But many of the husbands had surrendered the prime real estate of the bar area to the bulls and their wives and had retreated in small gaggles to watch from a safe distance. Seeing someone he recognized from a previous party, Alan took his ginger ale and made his way to a group of three men in their forties about ten feet away. "Hi, er, I think we met here a couple of weeks ago," he said, starting to extend his hand, then thinking better of it. He lowered his eyes half-way through the greeting. "I'm Alan."

"Yes, I remember. You're with that gorgeous tall brunette, right?" He was looking at Susan, who now had her arm around Richard's broad shoulders while the two of them talked to another of the black bulls at the bar.

"Well, she's with her bull right now, but yes."

"I'm Gene. That's my wife at the bar," he said, gesturing toward a stout blond whose generous breasts were spilling out of her unbuttoned blouse. She was leaning into a kiss with a man who was about two inches taller than her. His hand was moving slowly along the contours of her amply shaped behind, which was barely covered by a skirt that seemed to Alan too short for a woman of her physique. "They met about half an hour ago. I'd say they're getting along well," Gene said with a mischievous wink. As he said this, the man pulled back from his kiss with Gene's wife, whispered something to which she nodded, and they put down their glasses, hands entwined, and walked toward a door at the back. As they passed Gene, his wife gave him a discreet nod, curling her lips ever so slightly into a smile.

Alan wondered if Gene would follow them, but he turned back to their conversation. "We come here pretty much every Saturday," he said. It started as a punishment for me. My wife found out I was screwing this woman at work. I do deliveries and I was screwing the dispatcher in this quiet little corner of the warehouse. She used to dispatch me with these amazing blowjobs!" He laughed at his own joke. "When my wife found out, she was furious. She'd heard about this place from a girlfriend, and she told me that, if I wanted to stay out of divorce court, I'd bring her here and let her pick a guy up and fuck her brains out. Part of the punishment was that I'd have no say in who she fucked, and I'd have to watch. I had to promise to bring her here twice.

"The first time she went straight for this tall black guy" Gene continued. She knows I don't like blacks – no offense, you know – and I think that's why she did it. I had to stand here and watch him, black as coal, pawing her at the bar, licking those big fat lips of his as he eyed her up. I think the races should keep to themselves, that's the way it's supposed to be, but I had to sit there in one of those rooms in the back, so close

Alan looked at his wife who was dancing to a slow number with Richard. His hand was roaming beneath her skirt. Won't be long now, he thought. He decided to wander into the back to see what was happening before watching his wife with Richard.

his butt was practically in my face, so close I could smell his sweat, watching him fuck her. He had this enormous cock – it really is true what they say, you know – and she made a point of sucking it for what seemed like hours, and I had to just sit there and watch. Then when he fucked her – you know, he came three fucking times! What is he, some sort of sex machine? – she kept telling him how big his cock was and how great it was to be fucked by a real man. I tried to get up and sneak out. I thought she wouldn't notice, what with how loud she was moaning and all, but she was right on it. 'Don't you go anywhere!' she said. 'You're going to watch how a real man fucks me.'"

Alan looked over to his wife, who was now being led to the dance floor by Richard, and felt something tighten in his loins.

"After that, I made her promise, no more blacks, if we came back here. The second time she picked up this Asian guy. I was surprised how big his cock was, for an Asian guy. And I also realized that it kind of turns me on, watching the missus with another guy. So we've been coming here most Saturdays for the last six months. She's happy, I'm happy. No more talk of divorce. And sometimes I get a little pussy here myself.

"Anyway, gotta go. It's been about five minutes. She likes to settle in with a guy before I show up, but she gets pissed off if I miss too much of the action. I once let her go in the back with this guy she'd met here before, then I tried my luck at the bar instead of watching her. Man, was she pissed off at me! "You're not here to get laid. I am!" she said." He paused. "I imagine she has his cock in her mouth by now. She won't be happy if I get there after he starts fucking her. She likes me to watch when the other man puts his cock in her for the first time."

And with that, Gene ambled off toward the door at the back.

Alan looked at his wife who was dancing to a slow number with Richard. His hand was roaming beneath her skirt. Won't be long now, he thought. He decided to wander into the back to see what was happening before watching his wife with Richard.

Alan threaded his way past the dozen or so couples dancing on the floor. He was facing a door on which a sign said "do not enter if nudity offends you." He opened the door into the familiar narrow corridor lined with rooms on either side. The music faded to a quiet throb as he closed the door behind him. The predominant noise now was of sex as the moans of women in videos and actual women from the club mingled and drifted along the corridor.

The first room on the right was the gloryhole room. Four neat little holes were cut in the wall and there were cushions on the floor. A separate door, for men only, led to a space on the other side of the wall. The room was empty now but, as the night drew on, women would be kneeling on the cushions, servicing anonymous cocks of all sizes with their hands and mouths. The cocks would belong to the bulls who had struck out at the bar and to some of the husbands whose wives had gone off with other men.

As Alan moved along the corridor, there were rooms on either side, each with a modest bed, a chair, a video screen, and a waste bin for all the tissues and used condoms that would be generated by the night's libertine activities. Some of the doors were closed and, as Alan walked by, he heard behind this door "oh God, that feels so good. Don't stop!" and, behind that door, "harder, harder, come on fuck me!" His mind tried to picture the women that went with their words, the positions they were in, the looks on their faces – and the looks on their husbands' faces.

While some women liked the privacy of the closed door, others enjoyed an audience and left the door open. Alan saw a group of three men clustered in one doorway and squeezed in to join them. Inside the room was Gene, the man he'd spoken with a few minutes earlier, sitting in a chair, rubbing a bulge through his pants. On the bed, his wife was on her knees, wearing nothing but stockings and bright red heels, her ample butt stuck high in the air, as she sucked the rock-hard cock of the man who had been groping her in the bar. She had one hand around the base of his cock, and was twisting it as she moved her mouth, lipsticked to the same color as her pumps, rhythmically up and down on his cock.

On the bed, his wife was on her knees, wearing nothing but stockings and bright red heels, her ample butt stuck high in the air, as she sucked the rock-hard cock of the man who had been groping her in the bar.

Shortly after Alan stepped into the doorway, Gene's wife, clearly enjoying the audience, pulled away and wordlessly rolled onto her back, spreading her legs to reveal a glistening pair of hairless lips. Her partner moved to his knees and pushed two long, bony fingers inside her as she grasped his cock, as if testing its firmness. Gene's wife smiled at her new partner, moaning quietly. After donning a condom with practiced skill, the man moved forward and placed his cock between the glistening lips, rubbing them with the tip. She said something Alan could not hear, then her eyes rolled and she gave a loud, involuntary moan as he plunged inside her. Alan looked over at Gene and saw him pulling down his pants to release a stiff, generously sized cock, which he was now rubbing as he watched the stranger take his wife. The men in the doorway, watching the bed as if in a trance, began to rub their crotches.

Soon the couple on the bed had struck a nice pace. As he held himself above her on strong arms, his buttocks clenching and unclenching as he pushed in and out, in and out, her breasts began to slap together with each stroke. Now her pelvis was rising to meet his thrusts. "Oh god, your cock feels so good. Fuck me harder!" she exclaimed as Gene looked on, his cock hardening in his hand. Gene watched with excitement as the man pulled her legs up, her heels resting on his shoulders, so he could thrust more deeply into her womb. She was now playing with herself with one hand, looking into his eyes and telling him to fuck her harder still as his thrusts intensified. Gene's cock spurted just as his wife yelled out, for all to hear, "God, I wish my husband fucked me like this!" This was just before she let out a piercing shriek and her body started shaking and twitching. Shortly afterwards, the man's buttocks clenched, holding his cock deep inside her, and he let out a low, long growl.

Snapping out of the voyeur's trance as the couple eased out of their embrace, Alan looked at his watch. He now realized it had been half an hour since he left his wife dancing with Richard. Susan would probably be cross with him. With mixed feelings he contemplated the possibility that she might be planning some punishment for him. He hurried back to the dance floor to look for her. A dozen couples were dancing to an 80s disco tune, but Susan was nowhere to be seen. Nor Richard. Damn! They were not supposed to fuck without him, but then he was not supposed to have left them for this long.

He went back through the door behind the dance floor, into the darkened maze of rooms in the back, to look for them. He looked into all the rooms with open doors. Some were empty, the unused beds looking somehow sad and flat. In others bodies of all ages and sizes were grinding at each other, rumpling and soiling the sheets, and titillating onlookers. Susan and Richard were not among them.

Now Alan felt his heart rate quicken. They were not supposed to be in a closed room, to lock him out. This was against the agreement, the agreement that was never spelled out but was as clear as an international treaty. Were they rewriting the agreement, the agreement that was nowhere written but was so clear? Alan began to pause outside the closed doors, listening to the moans from the other side to see if he recognized his wife's. No, that was too shrill and high, like the call of a tropical bird. He moved on. That one was too loud – like a Subaru against his wife's Mercedes purr. He hadn't realized before how finely attuned he was to his wife's sex sounds.

But now: what about this one? Yes, that might be his wife moaning behind this closed door. He touched the door handle, ready to plunge in. "But what if it's not her?" he asked himself. It was a serious violation of etiquette to open a closed door without permission. It could even get you thrown out of the club. He stood there, paralysed, listening to the quiet moans in search of sure recognition. Should he knock? Then he remembered that some rooms had peep windows. Did this one? He found the passage to the corridor that ran along the far side of the rooms, and found there were indeed two rectangular windows set high in the wall for this room. They were blocked by a blind operated by a machine that demanded dollar bills. He looked in his wallet. No dollar bills. He hurried back to the bar, got change for a twenty, then returned, now sweating and panting a little. His hands fumbled as he tried to force a wrinkled dollar bill into the machine, only to watch it rejected. He tried another, also rejected, then another. He heard the quiet metallic whir as the blind in the window went up. He squinted, getting used to the darkness in the room. On the bed lay a woman, eyes shut, mouth open, whose massive breasts and folds of stomach fat dominated the scene. Her legs were apart, a man's head buried between them. Alan was fascinated and repelled. He also now knew that he had not found his wife after all. Where could she be?

Then he remembered the studio. The studio was a new space they had been building. This would be the first week it was open. He retraced his steps back to the dance floor, and found the door off to the right. It was marked, simply, "studio." He opened it cautiously and found himself in a space the size of his living room. The far wall was made entirely of glass, and on the other side of the glass klieg lights illuminated a studio space dominated by a king-sized metal bed with railings on either end. He found himself alongside a couple and five or six men who were staring intently at the bed, on which his wife, naked except for her pull-ups and red heels, was on all fours being pleasured by two naked black men, one in front and one behind. The two men moved in rhythm with one another, both thrusting into her at the same time. A third man, white, was wandering around, clothed, filming the scene with a video camera. Had Susan even noticed that he'd arrived, or was she too lost in pleasure?

Alan immediately recognized the man thrusting into his wife from behind, his hands grasping her butt cheeks, as Richard. He had seen him take Susan this way many times before. But who was the other man, the vaguely familiar man whose cock was just buried between his wife's red lips, whose big hairy black balls were now being licked and sucked by his wife, whose body shuddered with every thrust from behind? Then Alan realized he was the man who had been talking to Richard and Susan at the bar. And the camera man was the bartender, whose shift had presumably ended. He was doing what Richard should have been doing, circling around the three naked bodies with his camera, in search of the perfect angles and close-ups. Behind the bed was a flat-panel TV on which the camera man's handiwork could be seen. The screen was so big that it made the men's cocks bigger than they were in real life. Alan felt the way he did at a hockey game, not knowing whether to watch the action itself or the larger-than-life images of it on the big screen. He half expected to see a playback of the best shots.

The door opened behind him and two more men wandered in to watch. Alan heard them say how much better it looked on a bigger screen and realized that the video of his wife with these two men was also appearing on TVs in the rooms on the other side of the dance floor. Everywhere, in almost every room throughout the club, people were able to watch his wife being taken by these two men.

Alan refocused on the scene in the studio. His wife was now rolling over onto her back and Richard was tying her hands to the bed railings behind her head with black ties. Richard knelt at one side of her head and fed his enormous cock into her mouth from the side while the other man knelt with his cock between her thighs and began to ease it between her engorged lips. Now Alan heard her moan loudly as the man whose name he did not know plunged into her as deep as he could, then pulled her legs in the air, her heels on his shoulders, as he pushed in and out with a steady rhythm. With her hands tied to the bed above her head, Susan could not pull him into her with her hands to his ass, nor could she grasp Richard's cock, which was no thrust more deeply into her mouth than Alan had ever seen. Given its substantial girth and length, Alan wondered how she was taking it without gagging. Richard was now lying across her face, fucking her mouth. The camera man brought the lens in close to catch the bulbous tip of his cock as it pulled almost free of her mouth, only to plunge back in again. Alan, confused, excited, transfixed, did not know whether to watch the knot of bodies on the bed, or whether to gaze at the oversized cock on the screen as it buried itself between those lips he knew so well.

Finally, Richard untied her and she sat astride the other man. Alan saw her cast a glance to the side, catch his eye, then turn back to whisper something to the stranger whose cock he could see thrusting up between the two magnificent globes of her ass. He watched as, over and over, the thick trunk of the man's cock became visible, the plastic rim of the condom showing at the bottom, only to bury itself once more up to the hilt. As they did this, Richard was probing her asshole with a long bony finger and this was driving Susan delirious. Her head was rolling and she was moaning loudly, calling out "yes, yes, yes!" Alan stood frozen, unable to move, as he watched Richard climb onto the bed, push Susan forward a little so her ass was sticking up higher in the air, and work his cock in there. Susan had never done this before and surely she could not take a cock as big as Richard's in her ass. Alan heard her protesting, "no, it's too big," but Richard kept slowly pushing it in, purring "there you go, baby, there you go." Then, it was as if some sort of resistance in her broke, and half of his cock was in, and she was screaming, but the screams, the like of which he had never heard from her before, were hard-edged screams of pleasure. Richard was moving slowly, only putting half of his cock into her ass, while the other man fucked her from underneath with more vigor. She was moving her pelvis up and down, up and down to meet each man's thrusts, screaming more loudly until her body began shaking all over and she slumped down, spent, on the man below. She lay on her back, eyes half closed, only half aware of what was happening, as the two men pulled out of her and knelt on either side of her, stroking their cocks until each spurted gobs of white onto her breasts. Alan now realized that some of the men around him had been stroking their cocks as they watched the scene. With nothing left to watch but three spent, sweaty bodies lying entangled on the brightly lit bed, the men began self-consciously zipping themselves back up and shuffling back to the door, ready to seek out the next scene elsewhere in the club. Feeling as if he were intruding on something private on the other side of the glass, Alan went back to the bar, ordered a whisky and waited.

The door opened behind him and two more men wandered in to watch. Alan heard them say how much better it looked on a bigger screen and realized that the video of his wife with these two men was also appearing on TVs in the rooms on the other side of the dance floor. Everywhere, in almost every room throughout the club, people were able to watch his wife being taken by these two men.

After about fifteen minutes Richard and Susan appeared, reinstalled in their party clothes. The other man was nowhere to be seen and Alan presumed he would never meet him. The bartender materialized behind Richard and Susan, a big grin on his face. He handed Alan something. The videotape!

"Enjoy!" he said.

Be subversive... Subscribe

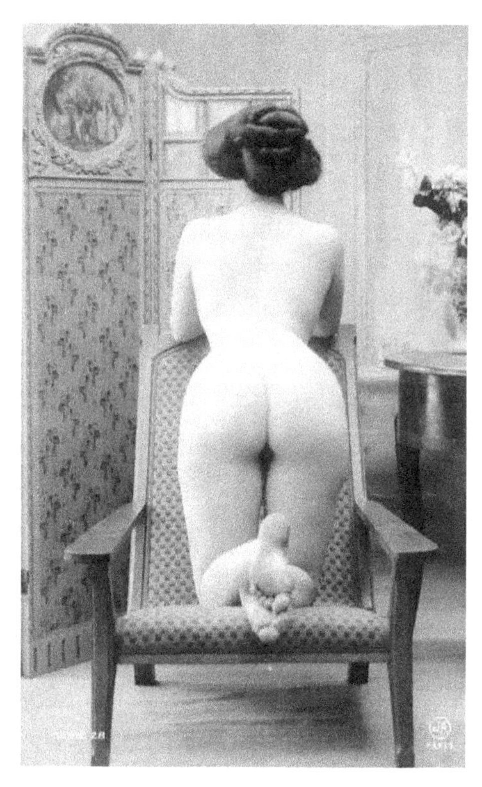

Want to save off the cover price? Consider subscribing to *THE ACT ITSELF* and SAVE!

Individual issues are available for only $14.95

Subscribe to three issues per year for only $40.00 and SAVE!

For more info, contact info@theactitself.com or write to:

THE ACT ITSELF
c/o BearManor Media
PO Box 1129
Duncan, OK 73534

or FAX
814-690-1559

Stay tuned to our website for news on audio and electronic versions of The Act Itself!

Convenient print subscription form:

YES! I would love to be subversive and order a 3-issue subscription to *THE ACT ITSELF*!

Name____

Street____

City ________________________ **State** ________ **Zip**________

___**Check** ___**Money Order** **(Please make check or money order out to BearManor Media)**

Mail to: THE ACT ITSELF, c/o BearManor Media, PO Box 1129, Duncan, OK 73534

EVERYTHING OLD IS NEW AGAIN

P.C
PARIS
2169

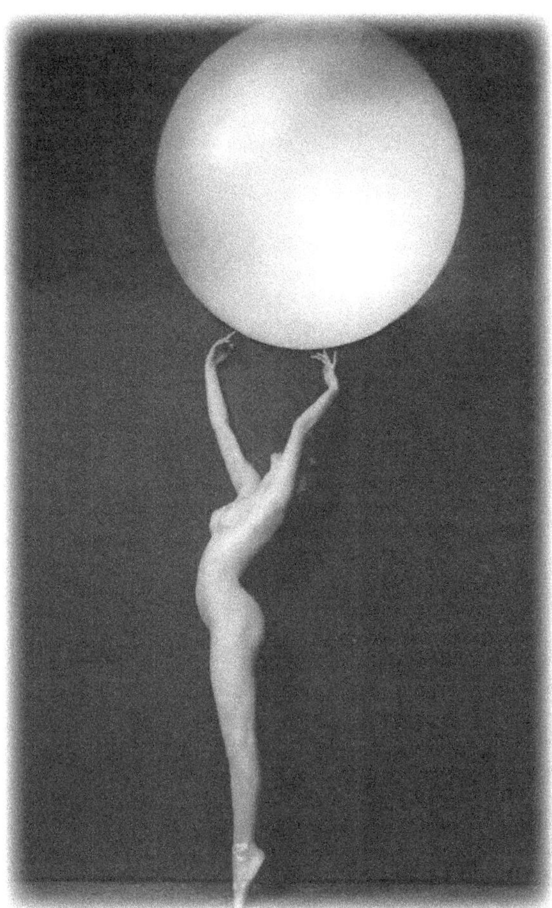

Corona
127

JB
26

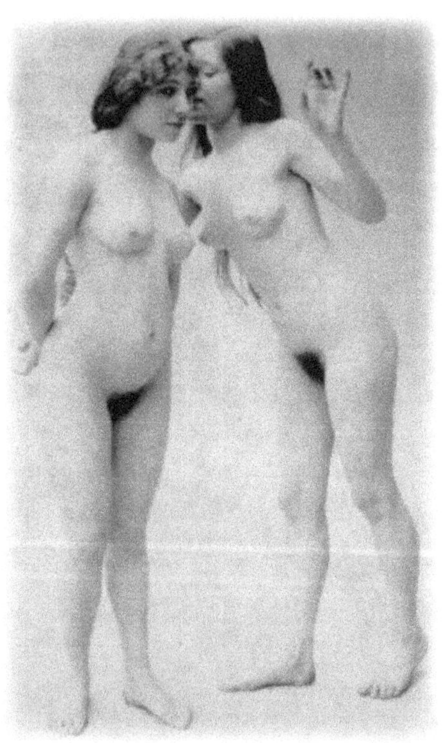

LIKE BROTHER & SISTER

by The Mrs.

It was late. Em's life changed when she awoke briefly and breathed deep and couldn't see some of the screen through her bulk. A wide but flat torso was there attached to blonde hair, telling her how much energy she had *now.* Em haunted a bag of jalapeno Combos slowly until her hand no longer came up to her mouth. She stopped in mid-crunch.

She ordered the Fat Whacker from the blonde. Followed the instructions – the accredited dietitian's diet was the hard part. But she dropped 28 pounds in two months. She had the abs of a 25 year old. She was her high school weight again. She was 58 years old.

She was thin.

Her children didn't like her, complaining that it was unhealthy to lose so much weight. They weren't worried for her, they were jealous. She glowed.

She was starting to insert *Marie Clare* magazines inside herself again. They smelled good, and they felt good. Ghosts returned. The remnants of feelings long since dead. Good feelings within. *Great feelings.*

Five months later, Jason called her into his office. He was frowning, and he never frowned. "Emily. Are you okay?" He sat his big black ass on the desk.

"I'm fine. What's up?"

"What's up?" He laughed. "You're starting to talk young people."

She blinked. "I said what's up when I was 12."

"That's pretty young, isn't it?"

"What's your concern, Jason?"

He put his hands on her wrists. Definite disciplinary action. She could have his job for that.

"I'm going to have to let you go."

"What! *Why?*"

He screwed up his screwed up face. He was an ugly nice guy. "There have been complaints."

"What? What did I do?"

He waited a while. "Can I be frank?"

"I don't care." She shrugged. Nothing made sense.

"That's pretty young, isn't it?"

"What's your concern, Jason?"

He put his hands on her wrists. Definite disciplinary action. She could have his job for that.

"Did you receive those notes I sent you?"

There had been many notes, mostly of a sexual nature. Em just threw them away, assuming none of them were for her.

Jason came closer, if that were possible, and patted her knee. Her bare knee.

"It's your choice of clothing," he said.

She looked at herself. Then at him. What?

He slid his hand into her dress.

"These legs go all the way up, don't they?" He laughed.

Em turned red. She hadn't felt a hand that high up since...

He was still talking, saying something, when she came out of it. His hands were in his fat lap and his fat lap was all over his brown Samsonite desk. She couldn't believe she ever had a spread like that.

"What's wrong with my clothes?"

He was surprised.

"Haven't you heard anything I said? *Did* you get my notes?"

"No."

"You didn't get any notes?"

"Not from you."

"What makes you say that? They were on your car, and on your desk, weren't they?"

Em shook her head. "They were the usual 13 year olds. Of a sexual nature."

Jason raised his big black eyebrows and took his glasses off. "Really? What did they say?"

"You can't do anything with them. They were unsigned and there's no way of knowing."

"But what did they say?"

"I can't remember exactly. They were love sick and sex starved."

"Like – 'I want to do you?' Like that?"

"Like that, but more explicit."

"Okay. Like... 'I would love to fuck your face and cum in your hair and make it stand up and stand you up and plug you like the bathtub, make you scream.'"

She looked at him. Him looming all over her.

Slowly, she said, "That... was one of them..."

He smiled at her. "Did you ever get a letter like that before?"

"Before what?"

"Ever."

She shook her head, and tried to remember if there was another chair in the room she could move to.

"That's because you're hot now, Emily. You've got the body every boy here wants to be in. I've had more than a few complaints about you wearing skirts, showing your ass when you drop an eraser. Things like that."

"I don't – !"

"I know, I checked, you wear panties." He grinned at her, which was different from his smile. "At least two mothers have called this office to complain that their son's homework was covered in... man stuff. One dad was laughing when he was talking about Taylor's iPhone being ruined, he'd have to get him a new one. Because his man stuff got all over it. He had pictures of you. *Lots* of upskirts. Too bad about his phone. Unless you keep them in a cloud, they're lost. Can't transfer pix from one phone to another.

"Well, the dad was forced to call and complain because I guess his wife couldn't bring herself to complain about that."

She was listening with one ear. One eye was on Jason. It seemed like he was removing his jacket. Then his tie. But that didn't seem right.

"Some of the boys are... masturbating to – me?"

The principal blinked a *yes*, and unbuttoned the first two buttons on his shirt, feigning hotness.

"Not just the boys."

"*The girls*?" She shook her head. "I can't believe that. No... I don't! My clothes aren't any more... risqué than anything I see walking through the halls."

"Yes, but they don't have a dress code. We *do*. It's hot in here..."

"My clothes aren't..."

She couldn't find the word.

"*The girls*?" she repeated.

Jason nodded and sat his hulking pudge behind his desk. "Kylie Berry, for instance."

Em thought. "Well, she looks like a boy."

"That doesn't really matter. Oh, shit. That tack again. Hey, could you grab that big red tack there and put it back on the board. On the white part. It never will stick on the cork side."

Em slid out of her seat, in a bewildered state of mine. Trying to remember what the color red looked like. There it was. Tightly fallen between the wall and the towering filing cabinet that would never move. She put her hands on both sides, and bent way down. It was hard. The tack was so close to the wall.

Finally she got it and tacked it on the cork side. When she turned around, Jason was exercising. Perhaps. She sat. And her mind didn't focus on what was going on until the tip of his tall black cock started to edge its way slowly over the desk and upset a small stack of essay booklets.

She wasn't sure how to start... the conversation.

"What's going on?" she finally asked.

"I would love to fuck your face and cum in your hair and make it stand up and stand you up and plug you like the bathtub, make you scream!"

Em's eyes widened. Her mouth got open. She started breathing hard.

Jason looked at her bouncing naval. He *loved* a good midsection. He hasn't seen a legal one that fine, in person, in

He let out a moan she didn't understand and picked up the pace on his jacking.

"Just put your glasses on."

It seemed harmless enough. She wasn't smiling or encouraging or anything.

"Okay," she said to get his eyes open.

Now he looked at her, and never even blinked.

He twirled his neck around, flung his right hand a couple times to massage it in the air. When he was back to jacking, he said, "I bet you like sucking dick."

Em said nothing.

"Tell me something."

"What?" she asked.

"Do you like sucking dick?"

ages.

"Keep your mouth open. Just like that."

She closed it. Without thinking.

"No, can you put your finger in your mouth?" he asked breathily. "Like you're thinking. Just like you're thinking."

Her hand almost did it, involuntarily. She was hugely distracted.

When her hand stopped in midair, the principal yelled quietly, "No, keep going please. I just want to cum on these papers!"

"Jason! What are you..."

She knew exactly *what are you*... Especially after indignantly raising herself from her chair, and seeing that massive cock churning butter.

"I want to cum over that tummy..."

"What are you doing?"

"I want to fuck you in the desk. In a small desk..."

"Why are you..."

"Oh, you're so fucking hot, so fucking hot..." He repeated it to himself, eyes closed, until he came. And though she was standing four feet away, he got some on her standing knee.

He calmed. He smiled to the Lord. The sound of the bell signaling third period rang through his mind. Jason put his big hands flat on the desk. His papers were covered, and he loved it. Loved looking at them.

Then he saw her knee.

He grabbed his cock again like a rock microphone, and started making it into something bigger. It didn't take long, with what he was saying.

"I bet your pussy is so tight..."

"I've had three children."

"I bet that cunt is dripping..."

She wanted to feel complimented. Knew that she should. But it was all too fast. And it was third period. She had to –

"Just put your glasses on," he pleaded through half eyes.

The glasses she wore just to read were in her curly brown hair. Her hand went to them without thinking. Jason's self-hypnotism stalled her:

"I bet you like getting your teeth brushed, don't you, Emily? Say you do."

"I brush at night and in the mornings." She nodded.

"I'd like to brush your teeth."

It seemed harmless enough. "Okay."

He let out a moan she didn't understand and picked up the pace on his jacking.

"Just put your glasses on."

It seemed harmless enough. She wasn't smiling or encouraging or anything.

"Okay," she said to get his eyes open.

Now he looked at her, and never even blinked.

"Put your pinky in your mouth." She did. "Bite on the fingernail." Okay, she did that. "Put it in more now, slide it into your mouth all the way."

"No."

"Just to the second knuckle."

She did that.

He twirled his neck around, flung his right hand a couple times to massage it in the air. When he was back to jacking, he said, "I bet you like sucking dick."

Em said nothing.

"Tell me something."

"What?" she asked.

"Do you like sucking dick?"

Em said nothing.

"I bet you like getting your teeth brushed."

"We've established that."

She looked at her watch. She wished her first husband would've taken this long. But she learned long ago that marriage is that last thing you should do to your sex life.

It was strange. Seeing something so natural, so up close. She had forgotten such things existed. She assumed all the boys at Waft Jr. High were starting to play with themselves about now, but it had –

"I bet your breath smells like cum…"

But it had been more of an abstract idea, distanced by age and a lack of caring. It hadn't anything to do with her.

Were they really playing with themselves though? To *her*?

Jason seemed to prove that.

She

"Pearly white… pearly white…"

She wondered about those notes. Jason quoted one. Did he write them all, or did he get off on hearing about them, hijacking them? She'd have

Jason was leaning over her now, cumming in her hair. On her glasses. It dribbled so much for a second cumming. Em darted away, trying not to scream, trying not to gag at the memory. This was the smell of cum. She remembered now. Only in the back of her mind.

In the front, she wondered how she was going to wash her hair in a junior high with no showers.

While he scraped the cum from her eyelids, Jason had explained that he meant no disrespect. He just wanted to land on her bones.

She'd been given an extra sick day and a reminder that she only had 4 more years to retirement (unless she wanted to buy more years back; she'd bought back 2 more a few years ago). It would be a shame, he'd said, to give up her future for the sake of a few fucks.

Only a few, he'd promised. One or two. Three at the outside.

And he'd been explicit, as he found a hat to cover her hair cum, about what he wanted. First, he wanted to brush her teeth with his cock until he came. Whatever she wanted to do with the cum once it was in there, that was fine with him. Cum had protein... he read a little more from a college science book. (A well-prepared man, she thought, steaming through her head.) Next, he wanted to cum insider her while she was dressed like a cheerleader. She was past menopause (he thought) and so (reading from the text again), he told her how safe everything was. He'd never worn a condom in his life...

By then they were just words saying something.

The hat on her head felt like it was going to keep falling off. She was worried about that.

Em went straight home, forsaking her usual Tully's Coffee stop in favor of extreme thinking time.

Everything was extreme these days, she thought. When she laid into her kickboxing routine, she so kicked the shit out of her body bag. Working up a sweat, she never once thought of Jason as the bag. And that made her wonder.

As usual after a workout, to relieve muscle stress (the net said it's good to do this), she took a *new* magazine, rolled it up and inserted it. It felt good going in. That usual layered feeling of glossy pages was somehow so relaxing...

"Em?"

Too relaxing. When Bryant found her, she was still there. Cuddled up into a little naked ball. The mag, still partially inserted, and all wet with Em juice. The smell of perfume from the Nicole Kidman ads made it an interesting room to enter.

Her brother merely backed out, when he saw *that*. He knew she was going through life changes at the moment, and it didn't really throw him. Not too much.

He went out into the living room, slammed a few doors, then turned the TV on. Things he never did before.

He went into the kitchen and made some toast. Toast had a strong smell. Bacon was better, but he didn't know how to fix bacon.

"What the hell's going on?" Em yelled over the TV.

"Hey."

"Hey!" She turned the TV off and came into the room with blinking eyes. "What are you doing here?"

"I came to get some cans of something. What are *you* doing here?"

She told him. After a think. They'd always been honest with each other, and close, before he moved all the way up to Wisconsin for that log job. He was back now, for a week. But Bryant knew his sister had been too long divorced and unvisited by kids to ask him to stay in her big house. And she didn't ask him to stay. Only gave him a key so he could come over whenever he wanted.

Yes, she told him. But in a PG way. She wasn't sure how he'd react to the word "cum" and all those masturbatory statements Jason was making, half of which she couldn't remember now anyway.

"Jeez, Em."

"I know it. I couldn't believe it."

"I can't believe that!"

"I've got his DNA in the other room."

He waved his hands at her. "I don't wanna see that. Jeez! What are you gonna do?"

"What *can* I do? I'm asking you. What can I do?"

They each took an end of the reclining sofa but didn't recline. The TV was on. But wasn't it always?

"Turn that off," he told her. The remote was in her hand. It had been so automatic. Turning it on, watching. She paused for a long time after she realized that. Then, turned the tube off.

"Should I be worried about that?"

"Of course!"

Em shook her head, and reclined. "Turning the TV on."

"Huh?"

The words came out so slow it was like she was inventing them as she said them. "Maybe I'm sex mad. Maybe it doesn't mean anything to me."

"What are you talkin' about?"

"I just turned the TV on – "

"Forget that part," he told her. "You're breathin', ain'tcha?"

"So?"

"So, are you thinkin' about that?"

She thought about what happened to her. Then she tried to visualize the cum in her hair. It was getting farther and farther away from her. It wasn't exactly a smile, but something that came close was arresting her face.

"When's the last time you made love?"

"Oh, Bryant..."

"When's the last time you doodled yourself?"

"I can't draw!"

"Lookit here." And he took them out for TCBY. It was getting hot in here. Splitting a 20 oz. White Chocolate Mousse with Heath Bar seemed the only thing right.

They spoke of family things. How was Sissy's leg. What George was doing now that he had the hook on it. Elongating what they'd said before, when he'd first arrived. It seemed right. Natural. Em's face was finally glowing down. The nipples through her shirt weren't too visible anymore. Unless you looked for them.

They drove out to Chester's and had tiny chicken sandwiches, though Em took the meat out of hers. Then the bread.

"I admire that," he told her, as they got in the car. It was 7 and the wind was moving the clouds toward rain.

"What's that?"

"Sticking to your diet."

"It's not a diet. It's a lifestyle. It's a way of thinking now."

Bryant snorted and blew something into a hanky. "What way are you thinking?"

"Healthy."

He rubbed her shoulder and they drove for a while listening to Aerosmith on Lite 95 FM. There on State Road 43 was the old covered bridge neither of them had seen, neither of them being from here originally. But it was famous and rustic and a good area to sit a spell and count squirrels in the setting sun. A few were running along the roof. No one was using the bridge for driving.

"Whatcha gonna do about your boss?"

She'd been thinking about that. "What can I do? What would you do?"

"I say fuck 'im." And before she could think to respond, he said, "I mean... is he a bad smelling man?"

Thinking. Remembering. "No."

"You're too old to get pregged, Em. Was it fun? I mean, you're hot and stuff."

"That's not the point, is it, really."

"No. But –"

"He didn't ask me anything."

"Is that the real thing? You want to be sweet talked?"

"I don't want to be dick slapped, no."

"Did it hurt?"

"That's hardly the point."

Bryant smiled to himself, then gave her some smile. "I'm missing the points around here a lot lately." He rubbed his neck to have something to do.

Suddenly Em laughed. "You remember that time you and I were feeling each other in the pie shed?"

It wasn't so long ago. Only middle age minus youth. "I remember that. It smelled like pumpkin."

"What did?"

He leered at her. "You're a card."

They laughed, and looked at each other, and tears started to form. In their eyes, of course.

"What should I do, Bryant? I like teaching. I've been doing it too long to just – stop. I didn't figure on stopping. It's not fair."

"What's most important? No. I mean... you've got a killer body. Why don't you use it. Come on. The guy just wants to fuck you. I was thinking... I mean. Yeah. It was pretty shocking. I was shocked. But you there. Hell, I see the man's point. I'd throw one over you too if you weren't my sister."

She sat for a while. There was a woodpecker somewhere close.

"What are you saving yourself for?" he asked. "Cry rape if it starts to sit on you. Hell, sex is power. You'll find yourself on top, if you know what I mean. You try it once. I bet you're the one calling all the shots."

Tuesday was Tuesday. It always is. The only treatment for Monday, when it rolls around, was a Tuesday. Em had taken the Monday off, not because she was still in shock or afraid

"What's most important? No. I mean... you've got a killer body. Why don't you use it. Come on. The guy just wants to fuck you. I was thinking... I mean. Yeah. It was pretty shocking. I was shocked. But you there. Hell, I see the man's point. I'd throw one over you too if you weren't my sister."

She sat for a while. There was a woodpecker somewhere close.

for her life or pussy, but just because. A solid day to think – to go see a re-release of *Leprechaun 3* at the Adelphy – and gather what was left of her thoughts.

As usual, she got to school before the kids. Before the other teachers. Em was in charge of bagels and Panera opened at 6. She had the keys to the school, and could open anything but Jason's office. The one place she was most interested in.

By the time he arrived, she was sweating. Uncertain. When Jason ambled in at 7:05 he started pouring like a drink himself. It was going to be a *hot* one.

Em raised herself up from the waiting seat in the Vice Principal's office and looked at him. He fucking looked at her. She was dressed like a slut on VE Day. Like a *Vogue* model (to him). Slit up the middle of her skirt, shirt with buttons that didn't matter, coming down to just above her cunny lips. He could see Everything.

It all looked good.

"This is how it goes down," Em said, slanting to show a curve. Confident. Sunglassed. Condom in one hand. A single sheet of paper in the other.

"Emma!"

"Thanks," and her crow's feet smiled at him. "Sign this. We do it all."

She handed him the page, but he was distracted. Something told his consciousness that there was nothing but a single paragraph on it, with a line at the bottom. But his superego was all over the place.

Let's face it. Any man would sign anything at that moment in time, and Jason was that fat, hairy man. Em took the signed paper and seemed to slide it into her ass, wherever it went. Jason was still distracted as they moved into his office. And she did give him everything. Except the initiative.

"What do you want?"

"What do you mean?"

"What do you want me to do?"

He was heaving and breathing like he was personally baking bread. "Brushing your fucking teeth," he fucking said. And he did just that. Creaming her gums. She gurgled a little, pretending just a lot she liked it. Just a little: she did.

The power felt Enormous.

And it preambled the Greatest teaching day she ever had in her life.

"You wouldn't believe it!" she yelled at her brother over a Golden Corral dinner. Everyone was happy here. Em could have the salad and a cheat of taco salad; Bryant could beef up on ribs, potatoes, cornbread and a host of personal fat.

She was talking with a wide, laughing face, shoveling good things into herself with fat free Ranch atop. "He fucked me sidewides! Sideways! He came in my hair, again! And that was the third time, before the first bell!"

"Congratulations!"

"I couldn't believe I could do all that! It was amazing!"

"I'll bet it was!"

"He was like on top of me the whole time. He was wheezing and breathing, I thought he was going to drop dead! We were on the desk, sideways. The first time it was all in my mouth and it was gushing like watching a boat motor in the ocean. Up really close, you know?"

"Em."

"It was... well, it was just the most amazing time ever. Ever."

"That's great."

"I couldn't believe it. You were right. Power. Power, man. It was his juice, right, but I was all in control. And I could feel it. I made him tell me each time what he was going to do to me. No more surprise. No more..."

"Em."

"Hmm?"

"I've got a boner."

"What's that? Are you choking?"

"No. I mean what you're saying's getting me hard."

"Oh." She finished chewing. "I'm sorry."

"Well."

"I was just so excited. You know?"

"I know! And I feel for you."

"I'm sorry. What did you do today?"

"I went to Walgreens."

He did. He went there for *Men's Fitness*, and actually bought the penultimate copy. Plus *Fit*. And *Fitness*. The smiling women on the covers all reminded him of Em. He came all over the covers; really messed them up. Bryant always had been a bit of a Peter North.

He left Jamie Foxx alone on *Men's Fitness*. Just opened up page after page and compared himself to the beefcake therein. Especially the lower halves. He was always all right in the arms and below the knees. It was sliding down below the tits that always caused confidence problems.

"What did you get at Walgreens?"

"Just some water and cards."

"What kind of cards?"

"Just some cards for Thanksgiving. That's our big season, even more than Christmas. The Dollar General closed up there at Jose."

"Really?"

"I can't buy anything for a dollar these days unless I go clear to Cordeal, and then you're talking gas money."

"You can't save anything that way."

"Em."

"Hmm."

"I'm still really hard."

They finished their buffet in silence. And as buffets really can't be completed, the silence continued, following them home.

So did Bryant's cock. It wasn't big or much of a dick, but six inches is six inches when it's there in brown jeans and you both know it's there.

Em rolled the Ford up to his Extended Stay. He couldn't drive because he couldn't rent a car from another state unless he had a credit card and he only had debit cards

"Could you suck it a little?"

"Bryant!"

He laughed. "I'm kidding! Don't worry about it."

Em laughed too. But her eyes were on it. She was hardly hungry. She looked at him, feeling a little sad.

"Just figuring..."

"What?" she asked.

"You."

"What about me?"

with him and the rental place required three in-state names and addresses for renting a car without a credit card – well, it's a long story.

"I'm sorry about your dick, brother dear."

"Don't worry about it."

"You haven't been taking Viagra, have you?"

"This is all word born, I assure you."

They tried to smile about it and they sort of did.

She shut off her lights and Mancini was playing a Pink Panther soundtrack on the college jazz station, she noticed. "Can I do anything?"

"Don't worry about it."

"Does it usually last this long?"

He laughed. "I can't remember!"

"I've got some Advil in the glove compartment. But it might be expired by now."

"Don't worry about it. It'll pass. Take a hot shower and shrivel."

"Can I do anything for you?"

This time there was a lull. *Revenge of the Pink Panther* didn't quite cover it.

"Could you suck it a little?"

"Bryant!"

He laughed. "I'm kidding! Don't worry about it."

Em laughed too. But her eyes were on it. She was hardly hungry. She looked at him, feeling a little sad.

"Just figuring..."

"What?" she asked.

"You."

"What about me?"

"And that lucky guy."

"Who? Oh, Jason? Well, I got four weeks in Tahoe out of that. I feel like a real whore."

"Oh god. Em. Really. Could you just..."

"What?"

"Where is Tahoe?"

"It's in California."

"That sounds like fornication. Everything is reminding... I mean... I can see your navel, for Christ's sake."

Em looked down at herself. She'd changed from her teacher garb for most of the day. But what she wore still proved she has a beginning, middle and end. Those legs.

"Yeah, your legs are pretty great. No veins at all."

"I have some veins."

"Could you suck my dick, Em? Just for five minutes. That's all."

"Ha!"

"I'm... sort of serious."

"Do you know how long five minutes is?"

"I'm not going to beg for five seconds. That's like... wetting your finger for wind direction. Five seconds isn't long at all."

She smiled at him. She remembered him putting his finger in the air when they went fishing at Stoppard's, near Greenwich. She was 9 and all the kids thought fish swam with the wind.

"I'm not going to suck anyone's dick."

"Five seconds."

She looked at him, hard. "Do you know what you're asking?"

"Asking you to suck cock." They each waited. "You've got all that pussy going to waste. You're not *doing* anything with it."

Laughing, Em looked around. Was anyone seeing this? Was this for real?

"Doing anything..." she muttered. "Why would you..."

"Who wouldn't?" Bryant shrugged. He opened the car door. The light was like a wake-up call to Em. He closed it again. They were in darkness. "Who's going to know?"

"No."

"I'm not asking you to get a table at Chick-fil-A." He opened his pants. "Put your hand on it."

She did. Not really realizing... "It's not very big."

"I know! It'd be like sucking wind. Well..."

She laughed, once. "I know what you mean."

"Come on..."

Em bent down. She opened her mouth. "It's pretty ugly."

"I know."

"Ew, there's a hair growing out of the side!"

"And it's going to smell like printed paper, come on."

She opened her mouth, and just before reaching the head, she stopped and said, "I'm only doing this to soothe you."

"I know."

"There's something wrong with it. I hope this..."

She sucked dick. Sucked it long and slow. Her throat muscles remembered... They remembered how to take a shaft and let it climb down her food hole until there just wasn't anywhere else to go.

The hair tickled her throat, and she almost gagged.

And she had to sneeze.

She pulled out quickly.

She opened her mouth, and just before reaching the head, she stopped and said, "I'm only doing this to soothe you."

"I know."

"There's something wrong with it. I hope this..."

She sucked dick. Sucked it long and slow. Her throat muscles remembered... They remembered how to take a shaft and let it climb down her food hole until there just wasn't anywhere else to go.

Not quite ready, Bryant took the damn thing in hand. Pumped it. Pumped it hard and often and consistently and thought of magazine women and stared at Em's middle.

"I need you to do something for me," he said.

"Shall I go get the police?"

"The police!" He came. He shot out and it clear reached the windshield. It sprayed the windshield.

And as it was spraying and painting and fogging up the view with liquid, Em opened her mouth and thought of firemen. Firemen saving lives and doing hatchet jobs and spraying buildings. And she was suddenly proud of her brother.

They didn't speak for two days. Neither called the other. Em taught. But taught Jason nothing new. He was not happy about Tahoe, and had to spend some quality time working that into next year's budget. Even though Em already got her ticket for Columbus Day week, just 10 days off.

Em went to Gold's Gym and pumped iron and glided like a skier, and watched all the beautiful people treat her with respect. Here, she felt like an equal. They smiled at her, nodded and held towels out for her and generally learned her name.

It was a little bit of fabulous.

So her confidence grew. She talked to the men who prowled the after-5 crowd. She went out with a Laurence. Then a Gaylord. That was a first. She sucked Gaylord's dick after the first coffee at his pad. Em knew window work, from a life before teaching, and Gaylord's windows were expensive. She sucked his cotton-smelling dick.

She went to Tahoe alone but never slept alone. It was the first time in her life she'd been so… wanted. Every man who wasn't obviously married spoke to her. The married ones too. She dated a wildebeest of a man for two whole nights who walked around with his shirt open, talked with a spirited, spiked accent and made love like a gigolo on coke. The actual two minutes was disappointing, but the activity up until then was a hoot.

She had a threesome with a pointy rich man in his top floor hot tub. Everyone looked down at the city from top of the Marriott as they individually got off, and he gave monogrammed mints to everyone as they left.

Thursday she had her first taste of Native American cock, which didn't taste like anything, and enjoyed a private nude beach with a man who made the parts for machines which made tractor parts. She went to sleep on the sand, rolled over, and he was on top of her before she could say fuck it. He kept finding the wrong hole, but they both had patience. And she got a white Gucci dress out of it.

Getting back to Orte, Montana was nothing if not nothing. It was lazy. It was sunny, in a gray way. School was beautifully boring and the kids were suddenly less than enamored with anything she ever did.

The gym called. The soft living had gotten into her pants and painted her abs the wrong color. It took solo dedication and a week of not eating to get close to smoking again.

59 was rolling around. Another year older. Em wondered if her brother was going to stay through the week to wish her one away from 60. THAT was the year she was dreading. And it was coming in just over 12 months.

Em drove to the Extended Stay and went into the office, asking for him. He was still there. He rarely left, the balloon of a night manageress suggested. Em grabbed a couple Aquafinas for them from the machine and knocked on Bryant's second floor door.

A whore answered the door politely. "Yes?"

"Oh, I'm sorry."

Bryant could see her from the edge of his rolling computer chair. "Em!"

"What's going on?" she asked, scuttling into wonderland before the door closed. Everyone was wearing g-strings, but Bryant merely looked bewildered, as if this was his very first second being here as well.

"Where have you been?"

"What are you doing?" his sister asked. The four or five girls were trying to get this new girl in bed and undress her. Em tried to be nice enough but clutched to keep her things on.

"You won't believe me."

"I know that!"

"This isn't my room."

"The manager seems to think so," Em said.

"No, no, it's not."

"She says you never go out."

"You want to get a breath of..."

It was one of his quirks, not completing the most important of sentences. And he could tell by her face that Em was very upset or jealous or angry or...

He closed the door, and the two of them stood bent over the railing looking over the outline of the mountain range in the distant darkness.

"Those girls are awfully quiet," Em said at last.

"Aren't they?"

"I didn't know you were into that."

Bryant didn't answer for a while. "I like whores," he said simply.

"Whores!"

"Well."

"What are you doing, Bryant?"

"There's a room capacity element to the proceedings... They get loud before I get off, they get out. You know how it is."

"I don't know!"

"Can we go somewhere?"

"I'm not going to suck your dick."

He had to laugh at that. "You're sex mad. You're looking..."

"I gained a couple pounds."

"That's it!"

"Shut up."

"Maybe you look better."

"I don't."

"Let's go to Red Lobster."

All the seafood there was far, far from the sea, but it was good and the cheese biscuits were worth the price of admission. After that, they just drove around looking at mountains. The conversation was getting back to normal. Relaxation fell on them to such an extent that Em felt she could ask what she wanted, the right way.

"What's with all the poontang?"

Bryant laughed a good minute with that, so she stopped the car and looked at his crotch. "I like poontang! Where did you hear that?"

"Kids today have words for everything, and they dig the old as well as the new. The more words you have – "

"I'll bet they've got a lot of words for you."

"What are you doing?" his sister asked. The four or five girls were trying to get this new girl in bed and undress her. Em tried to be nice enough but clutched to keep her things on.

"You won't believe me."

"I know that!"

"This isn't my room."

"The manager seems to think so," Em said.

"I'll bet."

"Have you heard any?"

"Let's not start that."

"I won't get hard. I promise."

"You can't *promise*."

"I came ten times tonight already, Em. Don't worry about it."

"I worry about it." She faced him. "I worry about having sucked your cock. And not really feeling anything."

"Nothing?"

"I should feel pretty nasty or something. And it wasn't like love blinded me. I mean, I don't feel anything one way or the other."

"Okay. That's fine."

"That's probably not fine."

"Then it's okay to suck my dick again. Or let me fuck you. Why not?"

"Whoa. Whoa. You are." She looked away. "You are saying after ten times!" She looked again. And laughed, at him. "Are you serious?"

"It doesn't have to be tonight."

"No."

"Look."

"Forget it."

"Look, Em, you've got a birthday coming up."

"I don't want a fuck."

"*No*. I got you a sweater from Stein Mart."

"Where's that?"

"You can order online."

"Okay."

"And I got you a gift card from there, because I thought it'd be your style."

"Thanks."

"Happy birthday!"

"Thanks."

"So for your birthday," he said. "I figure. You can fuck me, then there will be no hard feelings when I leave. Everything will be fine. And that's a gift to you."

"*How* is that?"

"Look at how we are *now*. You said sucking my dick didn't mean a damn thing. One way or the other."

"You're a philosopher."

"No. I'm just giving us an out."

Em's voice turned a little older. A little more frail. "Brother. Dear. You had all that delicious young pussy. Why do you want what I've got? It doesn't make sense."

"I love you, Em."

The emotion went straight for her nose. It itched instantly. And made her eyes crease. It all happened so suddenly. Her entire face was red, like a headache was coming on. There was pressure under her eyes. She just wanted to bawl like a stepped on baby.

She hugged him. He clapped her on the back. And smoothed out her red dress, rubbing it up and down. He did it again. Then under her shirt. His arm moved around to the front and he cupped her breast right out of its bra pocket. The tit fell to the earth in his hand, but then his hand went lower. To the good stuff. The abs. The pussy. He scooted her a smidge and indexed her hole. She was still tight, god bless her.

And he was hard, and had shaved that hair off, god bless him.

OH, SABINE

Photos by Michiru

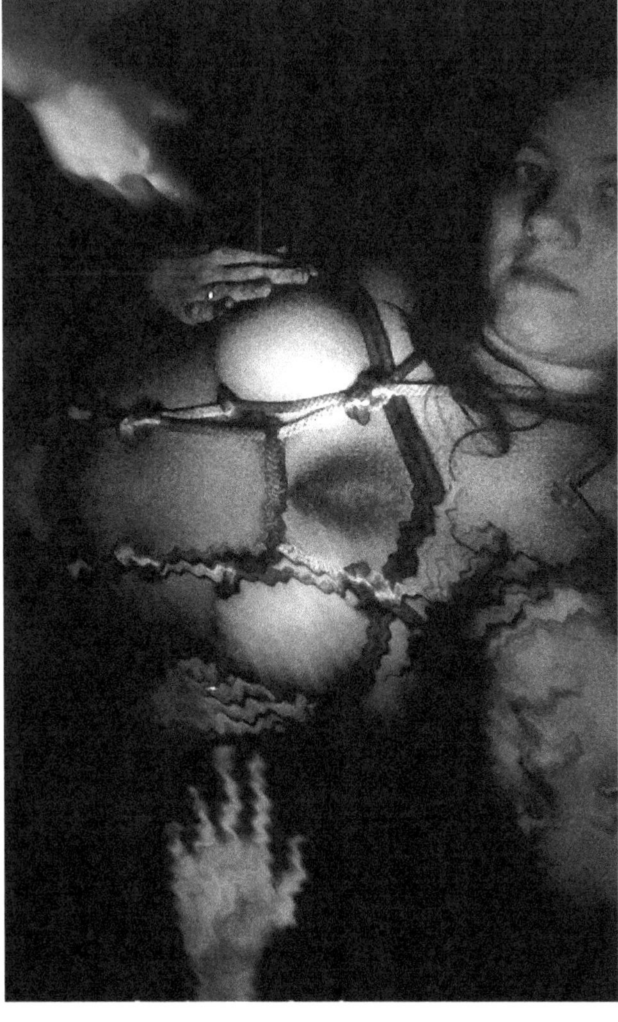

Michiru is a talented artist who has been involved in the fetish world for over eleven pleasureful years. She is also an accomplished writer, enjoys Japanese arts and cullture.

WRITING DOWN THE INCHES

by Jill C. Nelson

On August 8, 2008, my co-author Jennifer Sugar and I launched our first book, a porn biography titled *A Life Measured in Inches*, dissecting the life and times of adult film icon and pop culture figure John Curtis Holmes. As the first and definitive bio on the infamous porn superstar, we had expected to generate a great deal of interest and curiosity, and searched for a suitable location to hold our release party. Anticipating a full house, we were fortunate to have secured one of the most desirable venues in Los Angeles, the eclectic and renowned bookstore, Book Soup, located on Sunset Boulevard. Special guests that evening consisted of some of the most legendary and notorious personalities in the history of the golden age of erotic films: Ron Jeremy, '70s starlet Rhonda Jo Petty, Holmes's widow Laurie Holmes, Johnny Wadd film director Bob Chinn, and former adult performer Don Fernando. This was a first, in which fans, the media, and the stars convened for a few hours to chat, sign autographs, and mingle while sipping libations and eating a specially crafted cake meticulously replicating the front and back covers of our book. The official MC that evening was none other than William Margold, an adult film historian and self-designated Papa Bear who oversees his "kids" and hands out personal business cards that read, "God created Man, Bill Margold created himself." Margold wrote the foreword for our book, and delivered a heartfelt, funny, and crude introduction that night prior to inviting Holmes documentarian Cass Paley, Bob Chinn, Laurie Holmes, and finally Jennifer and me to take the podium to read book excerpts, answer questions posed

by the media, and meet fans. Jennifer also read a special letter submitted by one of our interviewees, the Platinum Princess, Seka.

For two first time female writers twenty-five years apart in age, living in different countries, who "met" only a few years previous on an imdb message board for the film *Wonderland* (a depiction of a robbery and murders in which John Holmes was involved), it was an exhilarating evening. The event culminated four years of research, more than thirty-five interviews, and the screening of over two hundred porn films. To industry insiders and outsiders, with zero background or knowledge of the world of pornography, Jennifer and I were probably two of the most unlikely people to pen a biography about the most notorious and "biggest" male porn star of x-rated films.

Jennifer, a 21-year-old MSU student pursuing a math degree, decided to write the first and definitive bio on Holmes in 2004 after having seen the film *Wonderland*, the same film that had drawn both of us to the imdb message board. Two years into her project, Jennifer had already completed several interviews, but realized that in order to bring her massive task to fruition she would require a collaborator. In the summer of 2007, after inviting me to come on board, Jennifer and I arranged a round of interviews in Los Angeles. It would be the first time we met up in person – just six months after our partnership began.

I recall that first morning in July. After having driven the one-hour trek on the freeway in my rental car from my hotel, I pulled up in front of a small house in Huntington Beach where Jennifer was staying. Apart from exchanging emails, chapters in development, and photos of one another, neither one of us had a true sense of what the other was like, or whether we were whom we had each claimed to be. After all, internet message boards are a little like online dating sites, you never know how much of the information being conveyed is truth or fabrication, designed to create an illusion of an individual who is trustworthy and safe. Trust was a major theme in this book's creation, and fortunately, neither one of us turned out to be ax murderers. In fact, after Jennifer and I shared a brief hug and she got into the car to return to Los Angeles with me for a few days, we laughed about some of the crazy scenarios each of us had devised in our minds prior to our official meeting.

Trust was a major theme in this book's creation, and fortunately, neither one of us turned out to be ax murderers. In fact, after Jennifer and I shared a brief hug and she got into the car to return to Los Angeles with me for a few days, we laughed about some of the crazy scenarios each of us had devised in our minds prior to our official meeting.

We had two interviews set for that day. The first was lunch in Hollywood with former LAPD homicide detective Frank Tomlinson and his wife Dianne. A self-described Biblicist, Frank, along with partner Tom Lange had been one of the key detectives in the Wonderland investigation back in 1981. Tomlinson was responsible for tracking John down in Florida, after he'd skipped town and gone underground for a period of six months. Tall and intimidating with piercing blue eyes, Frank was also friendly and kind, but after being burned by the media in the past, he made it clear from the outset that he would control the tone and length of our interview, and requested that we quote him verbatim. Frank asked that we refrain from asking questions, and instead, pressed the record button on Jennifer's small cassette tape recorder when he was ready to begin talking. A spell binding forty-five minutes later, he pushed the record button a second time, signifying that he was finished.

Later that day, Jennifer and I had scheduled a dinner interview with legendary film director, Bob Chinn, known primarily for creating and directing the famous Johnny Wadd film series starring Holmes as the charming and lusty, well endowed private detective Johnny Wadd. Long retired from the porn business, Bob was working in a camera shop in Culver City and suggested that we meet him at one of his favorite haunts, appropriately named Dear John's. Jennifer had already met and interviewed Bob once before on an earlier trip to California, but it was essential that we conduct a second interview in order to specifically understand the conception of the series and subsequent films, so that we could effectively screen and write reviews about the individual pictures.

Dear John's, a retro steakhouse and bar in Culver City, was not easy to pinpoint without a GPS. Eventually, we found it – a white and red brick standalone building located on a rather precarious curb. As we walked out of the bright sunshine and searing southern California heat into the darkened lounge about half past six, there sat Bob at

the bar sipping on a gin and tonic. The décor reminded us both of an old film set, red and black interior with a country and western singer crooning in the background, in and amidst the clatter of dishes and muted conversation.

Bob turned and waved when he spotted Jennifer before rising from the stool to escort us to one of the red padded booths. It was my first time meeting anyone famous in the adult film world in person, and I still wasn't sure what my preconceptions were. Spending those few compelling hours in Bob's quiet company, eating, having a couple of drinks and listening carefully as he thoughtfully and painstakingly answered all of our questions, I marveled at his impeccable memory and pinched myself that I was on board this ship.

The next morning was round two, a phone interview with Ron Jeremy.

Jill C. Nelson is the author of John Holmes: A Life Measured In Inches, *and* Golden Goddesses: 25 Legendary Women of Classic Erotic Cinema 1968-1985, *a collection of intimate portraits of 25 women who were involved in the adult movie industry during its golden age*

THE WAY OF A MAN WITH A MAID

Volume II, Chapter VI

by Unknown, 1908

A few days later I received a note from Mrs. Blunt saying that Alice was staying with her and she would be delighted if I would dine there with them quite quietly. I naturally accepted the invitation.

I was somewhat of a stranger to Mrs. Blunt. I had met her more than once and admired her radiant beauty, but no more. Now that there was more than a possibility that she might have to submit herself to me, I studied her closely.

She was more voluptuously made than I had fancied and was a simply glorious specimen of a woman, but she was something of a doll, rather shallow and weak-willed, and I saw with satisfaction that I would not have much trouble in terrorizing her and forcing her to comply with my desires.

During the evening Alice brought up the subject of my rooms and their oddity and made Mrs. Blunt so interested that I was able naturally to suggest a visit and a lunch there—which was accepted for the following day, an arrangement that made Alice glance at me with secret exultation and delighted anticipation.

In due course my guests arrived, and after a dainty lunch which drew from Mrs. Blunt many compliments, we found ourselves in the Snuggery. The girls at once commenced to examine everything, Alice taking on herself the role of showman while I, in my capacity of host, did the honours. I could see that Fanny was at her post of observation—and now awaited, with some impatience, the critical moment.

In due course Mrs. Blunt and Alice finished their tour of inspection and made as if they would rest for a while.

"What comfortable chairs you men always manage to get about you," remarked Mrs. Blunt as she somewhat critically glanced at my furniture.

"You bachelors do study your creature comforts—and so remain bachelors!" she added somewhat significantly, as she was among our deluded friends who planned a match between Alice and me.

"Quite true!" I replied with a polite smile, "so long as I can by hook or by crook get in these rooms what I want, they will be good enough for me, especially when I am permitted to enjoy the visits of such angels!"

"That's a very pretty compliment, isn't it Alice?" exclaimed Mrs. Blunt as she moved towards the Chair of Treachery which stood invitingly close, then gracefully sank into it.

Click! The arms folded on her. "Oh!" she ejaculated as she endeavored to press them back.

"What's the matter, Connie?" asked Alice, quickly hurrying to her friend, but in a flash I was onto her and had tightly gripped her. "Oh!" she screamed in admirably feinted fright, struggling naturally. I picked her up and, carrying her to the pulleys, made them fast to her wrists and fixed her upright with hands drawn well over her head, to Mrs. Blunt's horror! As I approached her. she shrieked, "Help ... help!" pressing desperately against the locked arms and striving to get loose.

"It's no use, Mrs. Blunt!" I said quietly as I commenced to wheel the chair towards the second pair of pulleys. "You're in my power! You'd better yield quietly!"

Seizing her wrists one at a time, I quickly made the ropes fast to them, set the machinery going and, just as she was being lifted off her seat, I released the arms and drew the chair away, forcing her to stand up. In a very few seconds she was drawn up to her full height, facing Alice, both girls panting and gasping after their struggle! "There, ladies," I exclaimed, as if well pleased with my performance, "now you'll appreciate the utility of this room!"

"Oh! Mr. Jack!" cried Mrs. Blunt in evident relief, "how you did frighten me. I was sure that something dreadful was going to happen!" With a poor attempt to be sprightly she continued, "I quite made up my mind that Alice and I were going to be..." she broke off with a silky, self-conscious giggle.

"I gladly accept the suggestion you have so kindly made, dear lady," I said with a smile of gratitude, "and I will do you and Alice presently!" She started, horrified, stared aghast at me as if she could not believe her ears. She seemed to be dumb with shocked surprise, and went deadly pale. I was afraid to glance at Alice lest I should catch her eye and betray her.

With an effort, Mrs. Blunt stammered brokenly, "Do you mean to say... that Alice and I... are going to be... to be..." She stopped abruptly, unable to express in words her awful apprehension.

"Fucked is the word you want, I think, dear Mrs. Blunt!" I said with a smile.

"Yes, dear ladies, as you are so very kind, I shall have much pleasure in fucking you both presently!"

She quivered as if she had been struck, then screamed hysterically, "No, no! I-I won't! Help! Help!... Help!"

I turned quietly to Alice (who I could see was keenly enjoying the trap into which Mrs. Blunt had fallen) and said to her, "Are you going to be foolish and resist, Alice?"

She paused for a long moment, then said in a voice that admirably counterfeited intense emotion, "I feel that resistance will be of no avail, but I'm not going to submit to you tamely. You will have to... force me!"

She paused for a long moment, then said in a voice that admirably counterfeited intense emotion, "I feel that resistance will be of no avail, but I'm not going to submit to you tamely. You will have to... force me!"

"Me also!" cried Mrs. Blunt, hysterically.

"As you please!" I said equably. "I've long wanted a good opportunity of testing the working of this machinery; I don't fancy I'll get a better one than you are now offering me, a nice long afternoon—two lovely rebellious girls! Now, Mrs. Blunt, as you are chaperoning Alice, I am bound to begin with you." And I commenced to unbutton her blouse.

"No, no, Mr. Jack!" she screamed in dismay as she felt my fingers unfastening her upper garments and unhooking her skirt—but I steadily went on with my task of undressing her, and soon had her standing in her stays with bare arms and legs—a lovely tall slender half-undressed figure, her bosom heaving and palpitating, the low-cut bodice allowing the upper half of her breasts to become visible. Her flushed face indicated intense shame at this indecent exposure of herself, and her eyes strained appealing towards Alice as if to assure herself of her sympathy.

"Now I will give you a few minutes to collect yourself while I attend to Alice!" I said as I went across to the latter, whose eyes were stealthily devouring Mrs. Blunt's provoking dishabille. "Now, for you, dear!" I said, as I quickly set to work to undress her.

She very wisely was adopting the policy of dogged defiance and maintained a sullen silence as one by one her clothes were taken off her till she also stood bare-armed and barelegged in her stays. But instead of pausing, I went on, removed her corset, unfastened the shoulder straps of her chemise and vest and pushed them down to her feet, leaving her standing with only her drawers on, a sweet, blushing, dainty, nearly-naked girl on whose shrinking trembling figure Mrs. Blunt's eyes seemed to be riveted with what certainly looked like involuntary admiration!

But I myself was getting excited and inflamed by the sight of so much unclothed and lovely girl-flesh, so eagerly returning to Mrs. Blunt, I set to work to remove the little clothing that was left on her. "No, no, Mr. Jack!" she cried piteously as I took off her stays. "Oh!" she screamed in her distress when she felt her chemise and vest slip down to her feet, exposing her in her drawers only, which solitary garment, she evidently concluded from the sight of Alice, would be left on her. But when, after a few admiring glances, I went behind her and began to undo the waist-band and she realized she was to be exposed naked, Mrs. Blunt went into a paroxysm of impassioned cries and pitiful pleadings. In her desperation she threw the whole of her weight on her slender wrists and wildly twisted her legs together in the hope of preventing me from pulling her drawers off. But they only required a few sharp tugs—down to her ankles they came! A bitter cry broke from her, her head with its wealth of now disordered golden hair fell forward on her bosom in her agony of shame. Connie Blunt was stark naked.

I stepped back a couple of paces and exultingly gazed on the vision that met my eyes. Close in front of me was revealed the back of Mrs. Blunt's tall, slender, naked figure, uninterrupted from her heels to her up-drawn hands, her enforced attitude displaying to perfection the voluptuous curves of her hips, her luscious haunches, her gloriously rounded bottom, her shapely legs.

Facing her stood Alice, naked save for her drawers, her face suffused with blushes at the sight of Connie's nakedness, her bosom heaving excitement not unmixed with delight at witnessing the nudity of her friend and trepidation at the approaching similar exposure of herself. I saw from the stealthy gloating glances she shot at Connie that she was longing to have a good look at her but dared not do so, lest her eyes should betray her delight, so I decided to give her the opportunity. I went over to her, slipped behind her, passed my arms around her and drew her against me and, holding her thus in my embrace, I gazed at the marvelous sight Connie Blunt was affording to us as she stood naked!

She was simply exquisite! Her pearly dazzling skin, her lovely shape, her delicious little breasts standing saucily out with their coral nipples as they quivered on her heaving bosom, her voluptuous hips and round smooth belly, her pretty legs, her drooping head exhibited her glorious golden hair, while, as if to balance it, a close clustering mass of silky, curly, golden-brown hairs grew thickly over the region of her cunt, hiding it completely from my eager eyes! In silent admiration I gloated over the wonderful sight of Connie Blunt naked—till a movement of Alice recalled me to her interests. She was keeping her face steadily averted from Connie, her eyes on the floor, as if unwilling to distress her friend by looking at her in her terrible nudity.

"Well, how do you like Connie now?" I asked loud enough for Mrs. Blunt to hear. She shivered; Alice remained silent.

"Aren't you going to look at her?" Alice still remained silent.

"Come, Alice, you must have a good look at her. I want to discuss her with you, to have your opinions as a girl on certain points. Come, look!" I gently stroked her naked belly.

"Oh! Don't, Jack!" she cried, affecting a distress she was not feeling. Connie glanced hastily at us to see what I was doing to Alice, and blushed deeply as she noted my wandering hands, which now were creeping up to Alice's breasts.

I seized them and began to squeeze them. "Don't, Jack!" again she cried.

"Then obey me and look at Connie!" I said sternly.

Slowly Alice raised her head, as if most reluctantly, and looked at Connie, who colored hotly as her eyes met Alice's. "Forgive me, darling!" cried Alice tearfully, "I can't help doing it!" But her throbbing breasts and excitedly agitated bottom told me how the little hypocrite was enjoying the sight of Connie's nakedness!

"Now, no nonsense, Alice!" I said sternly, and I gave her breasts a twist that made her squeal in earnest and immediately rivet her eyes on her friend lest she should get another twist. And so, for a few minutes, we silently contemplated Mrs. Blunt's shrinking form, our eager eyes greedily devouring the lovely naked charms that she was so unwillingly exhibiting to us! Presently I said to Alice, whose breasts were still captives in

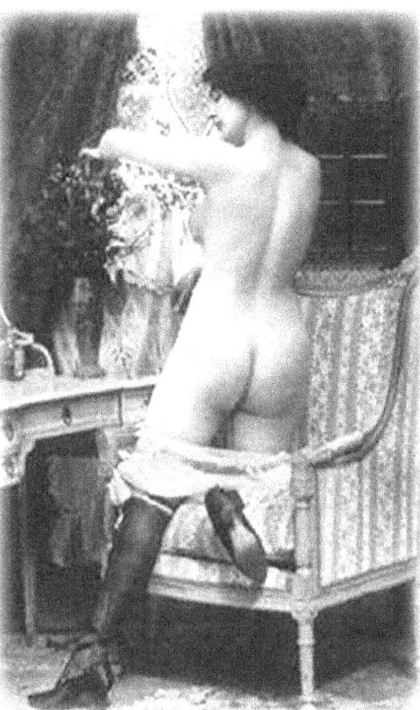

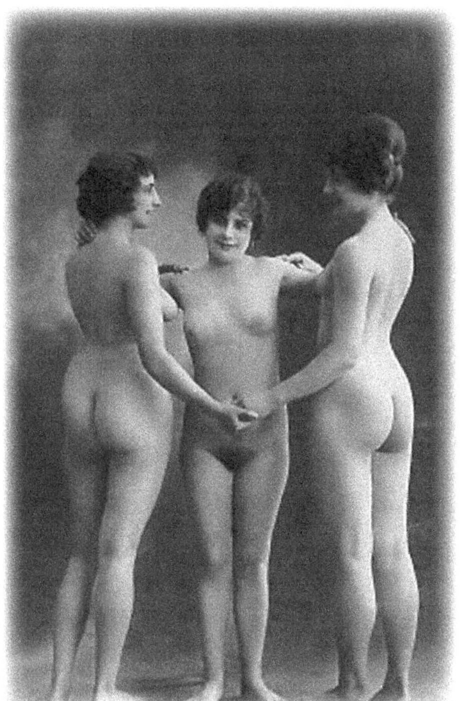

my hands, "Now, the plain truth, please—speaking as a girl, what bit of Mrs. Blunt do you consider her finest point?"

Alice blushed uncomfortably, pretended to hesitate, then said shamefacedly, "Her ... her ... private parts!"

Connie flushed furiously and pressed her thighs closely together as if to shield her cunt from the eager eyes which she knew were intently looking at it! I laughed amusedly at Alice's demure phraseology and said, "I think so too! But that's not what you girls call it when you talk together. Tell me the name you use, your pet name for it!"

Alice was silent. I think she was really unwilling to say the word before Mrs.

Blunt, but I mischievously proceeded to get it out of her. I gave her tender breasts a squeeze that made her cry, "Oh!" and said, "Come, Alice, out with it!"

Still she remained silent. I let go of one of her breasts and began to pinch her fat bottom, making her wriggle and squeal in grim reality, but she would not speak!

Seeing that Mrs. Blunt was watching closely, I moved my hand away from Alice's bottom and made as if I was going to pass it through the slit in her drawers.

"Won't you tell me?" I said, moving my hand ominously.

"Cunny!" whispered Mrs. Blunt in hot confusion.

"You obstinate little thing!" I said to Alice with a laugh that showed her that I was only playing with her. "Cunny!" I repeated significantly. "Well, Alice, let Mrs. Blunt and I see your cunny!"—and as I spoke, I slipped the knot off her drawers, and down they tumbled to her ankles before she could check them with her knees, exposing by their disappearance the lovely cunt I knew so well and loved so dearly, framed so to speak by her plump rounded thighs and her sweet belly.

I sank on my knees by Alice's side and eagerly and delightedly inspected her delicious cleft, the pouting lips of which, half-hidden in their mossy covering, betrayed her erotic excitement! She endured with simulated confusion and crimson cheeks my close examination of her 'private parts,' to use her own demure phrase! At last I exclaimed rapturously, "Oh! Alice, it is sweet!" As if overjoyed, I gripped her by her bottom and thighs and pressing my lips on her cunt, I kissed passionately! "Don't, Jack!" she cried, her voice half-choked by the lascivious sensations that were thrilling through her.

Seeing that Alice was perilously near to spending in her intense erotic excitement, I quitted her and went across to Mrs. Blunt, by whose side I knelt in order to study her cunt.

"Oh, Mr. Jack! Don't look, please don't look there!" she cried in agony of shame at the idea of her cunt being thus leisurely inspected by male eyes—and she attempted to thwart me by standing on one leg and throwing her other thigh across her groin.

"Put that leg down, Connie!" I said sternly.

"No, no," she shrieked, "I won't let you look at it!"

"Won't you?" said I, and drew out from the bases of the pillars between which she was standing two stout straps, which I fastened to her slim ankles in spite of her vigorous kicking. I set the mechanism working. A piercing scream broke from her as she felt her legs being pulled remorselessly apart, and soon, notwithstanding her desperate resistance and frantic struggles, she stood like an inverted Y with her cunt in full view!

"Won't you?" I repeated with a cruelly triumphant smile as I proceeded to blindfold her, she all the while pitifully protesting. I noiselessly set Alice loose and signaled to Fanny to join us, which she quickly did, stark naked as directed. The three of us knelt in front of Connie, I between the girls with an arm around each, and with heads close together delightedly examined her private parts, Alice and Fanny's eyes sparkling with undisguised enjoyment as we noted the delicate and close-fitting, shell-pink lips of her cunt, its luscious fleshiness, and its wonderful covering of brown-gold silky hairs! She quivered in her shame at being thus forced to exhibit the most secret part of herself to my male eyes.

I motioned to the girls to remain as they were, detached myself from them, leaned forward and gently deposited a kiss on Connie's cunt. Taken absolutely by surprise, Mrs. Blunt shrieked: "O-h-h!" and began to wriggle divinely, to the delight of the girls, who motioned to me to kiss Connie's cunt again, which I gladly did. Again she screamed, squirming deliciously in her fright. I gave her cunt a third kiss, which nearly sent her into convulsions, Alice and Fanny's eyes now sparkling with lust. Not daring to do it again I rose, slipped behind her noiselessly and took her in my arms, my hands on her belly!

"No, no, Mr. Jack!" she cried, struggling fiercely, "don't touch me! ... Oh-h-h!" she screamed as my hands caught hold of her breasts and began to feel them! They were smaller than Alice's, but firmer, soft, elastic and strangely provoking—most delicious morsels of girl-flesh. I toyed and played with them, squeezing them lasciviously to the huge delight of the girls, till I felt it was time to feel her cunt. Releasing her sweet breasts, I slipped my hands over Mrs. Blunt's stomach and her cunt.

"Oh! My God!" she shrieked, her head tossing wildly in her shame and agony as she felt my fingers wander over her private parts so conveniently arranged for the purpose. Over her shoulder I could see Alice and Fanny's faces as they watched every movement of my fingers, their eyes humid, their cheeks flushed, their breasts dancing with sexual excitement! From the fingers' point of view, Alice's cunt was the more delicious of the two because of its superior plumpness and fleshiness, but there was a certain delicacy about Connie's cunt that made me revel in the sweet occupation of feeling it.

Presently I inserted my forefinger gently between the close-fitting lips. The girls' eyes glistened with eagerness and they bent forward to see if Fanny's information was true, and I smiled at the disappointment expressed in their faces when they saw my finger bury itself in Connie's cunt up to the knuckle! She was not a virgin! But she was terribly tight, much more so than Fanny was when I first felt her, and Mrs. Blunt's screams and agonized cries clearly indicated that, for want of use, her cunt had regained its virgin tightness.

Keeping my fingers inside her, I gently tickled her clitoris in order to test her sexual susceptibility. She gave a fearful shriek accompanied by an indescribable wriggle, then another—then bedewed my hand with her sweet love-juice, her head falling on her bosom as she spent, utterly unable to control herself. I kept my finger inside her till her ecstatic crisis was over and her spasmodic thrills had quieted down—then gently withdrew it as I lovingly kissed the back of her soft neck and left her to herself.

As I did so, Alice and Fanny rose, their eyes betraying their intense enjoyment of the scene. With an unmistakable gesture they indicated each other's cunts, as if seeking mutual relief—but I shook my head, for Alice had now to be tortured. Quickly I fastened her up again while Fanny noiselessly disappeared into my alcove. I removed the bandage from Connie's eyes. As she wearily raised her head, having scarcely recovered from the violence of her spending, I clasped her to me and passionately showered kisses on her flushed cheeks and trembling lips. I saw her eyes seek Alice's as if to learn her thoughts as to what she had witnessed. Both girls blushed vividly as if in symphony. I pushed a padded chair behind Connie, released her legs and lowered her till she could sit down in comfort and left her to recover herself while I went across to Alice, who was now to be the prey of my lustful hands.

I motioned to the girls to remain as they were, detached myself from them, leaned forward and gently deposited a kiss on Connie's cunt. Taken absolutely by surprise, Mrs. Blunt shrieked: "O-h-h!" and began to wriggle divinely, to the delight of the girls, who motioned to me to kiss Connie's cunt again, which I gladly did.

But I was now in an almost uncontrollable state of lust! My erotic senses had been so irritated and inflamed by the sight of Mrs. Blunt's delicious person naked, her terrible struggles, her shame and distress during her ordeal, that my lascivious cravings and desires imperiously called for immediate satisfaction. And the circumstances that all this had taken place in the presence of Alice and Fanny, both stark naked, both in a state of intense sexual excitement and unconcealed delight at witnessing the torturing of Mrs. Blunt, only added further fuel to the flame of my lust. But to enjoy either Connie or Alice at the moment did not suit my program, and my thoughts flew to Fanny now sitting naked in my alcove and undoubtedly very excited sexually by Mrs. Blunt's struggles and cries!

Slipping behind Alice, I took her in my arms, seized her breasts, and said not unkindly while watching Mrs. Blunt keenly, "Now, Alice, it's your turn! You've seen all that has happened to Mrs. Blunt and how in spite of her desperate resistance she has been forced to do whatever I wanted—even to spend! Now I'm going to undress." Mrs. Blunt looked up in evident alarm.

"While I am away, let me suggest that you consult your chaperone as to whether you had not better yield yourself quietly to me!" I disappeared into my alcove, where Fanny, still naked, received me with conscious expectancy, having heard every word!

I tore off my clothing, seized her naked person and whispered excitedly as I pointed to my rampant prick, "Quick, Fanny!" She instantly understood. I threw myself into an easy chair. In a moment she was kneeling between my legs with my prick in her mouth, and she sucked me deliciously till I spent rapturously down her throat! Having thus delightfully relieved my feelings, I drew her onto my knees and whispered as I gratefully kissed her, "Now, dear, I'll repay you by frigging you, while we listen to what Alice and Connie are saying." Slipping my hand down to her pouting and still excited cunt, I gently commenced the sweet junction, she clasping silently but passionately as my active finger soothed her excited senses. From our chair we could clearly see Connie and Alice and hear every word they said.

Their embarrassed silence had just been broken by Alice, who whispered in admirably simulated distress: "Oh, Connie! What shall I do?"

Connie colored painfully. With downcast eyes as if fearing to meet her friend's agitated glances, she replied in an undertone, "Better yield, dear! Don't you think so?"

"Oh! No! I can't!" cried Alice despairingly, playing her part with a perfection that brought smiles from Fanny and me. With a change of voice she asked timidly, "Was it very dreadful Connie?"

Connie covered her face with her hands and replied in broken agitation. "I thought I should have died! The awful feeling of shame! The terrible helplessness! The dreadful position into which I was fastened! The agony of having a man's hand on my… cunny! Oh-h-hh!"

Fanny began to wriggle deliciously on my knees as she felt her pleasure approaching. Her eyes closed slowly; she strained me against her breasts.

Suddenly she agitated herself rapidly on my finger, plunging wildly with quick strokes of her buttocks. She caught her breath, murmured brokenly, "Oh-h-h!" and inundated my finger as she spent ecstatically! My mouth sought hers as, little by little, I slowed down the play of my finger in her cunt till she came to, deliciously satisfied!

Suddenly she agitated herself rapidly on my finger, plunging wildly with quick strokes of her buttocks. She caught her breath, murmured brokenly, "Oh-h-h!" and inundated my finger as she spent ecstatically! My mouth sought hers as, little by little, I slowed down the play of my finger in her cunt till she came to, deliciously satisfied!

"Now I'd better go to them," I whispered, and after a few more tender kisses I went out. My appearance, naked save for my shoes and socks, caused Mrs. Blunt to hurriedly cover her face with her hands as she hysterically cried, "Oh!… Oh!… Oh!"

I ignored her and took Alice into my arms as before and said to her encouragingly, "Well, dear, what is it to be?" whispering inaudibly in her ear, "You're to be tickled!"

Alice stood silent with downcast eyes. In her anxiety to hear Alice's decision, Mrs. Blunt uncovered her face and looked eagerly at us! At last it came! "No," spoken so low that we could just hear her.

"Oh, Alice! You are a silly girl!" exclaimed Mrs. Blunt, now afraid about herself. Alice cast a reproachful glance at Connie and said, almost in tears, the little humbug, "I can't! Oh, I can't!"

Without a word I fastened straps to Alice's pretty ankles and dragged her legs apart till she stood precisely as Mrs. Blunt had done. I carefully blindfolded her and seated myself just below her on the floor within easy reach of her, and began to amuse myself with her defenseless cunt, knowing that Mrs. Blunt could see over my shoulder all that passed.

With both hands I felt all of Alice's private parts, touching, pressing, stroking, parting her lips, even pulling her hairs every now and then, and peering into her interior—an act invariably followed by an ardent kiss as if in apology, she squirming deliciously. She submitted herself to the sweet torture in silence till I pretended to be trying to push my finger into her cunt, when she screamed in horror, "Don't, Jack, don't!" as if unable to endure it! "Hurts, does it, Alice!" I said smiling meanly. "Then I won't do it again! I'll try something softer than my finger!" After fetching a feather, I resumed my position on the carpet.

Alice's color now went and came and her bosom began to heave uneasily, for she guessed what was now going to be done to her, and although she rather liked having her cunt tickled, the existing conditions were not what she was accustomed to. She awaited her ordeal with a good deal of trepidation.

Quietly I applied the tip of the feather to her cunt's now slightly pouting lips with a delicate yet subtle touch. "O-h-h!" she ejaculated, quivering painfully. I gave her three or four more similar touches, after which she began to wriggle vigorously, crying: "Oh!... Oh!... Don't, Jack!" I was just beginning to tickle her cunt in real earnest when Connie, horrified at the sight, shrieked: "Stop!... Stop!... Oh, you awful brute!... You coward!... To torture a girl in that way!... Oh, my God!" she moaned, quite overcome at the sight of Alice being tortured!

How thankful I was that I had blindfolded Alice! I am sure that she otherwise would have given the game away—she must have laughed! In fact, some of her convulsions were undoubtedly caused by suppressed laughter and not by her torture!

"There's no better way of curing a girl of obstinacy than by tickling her cunt, Connie," I said unconcernedly, and I again commenced to tickle Alice.

"No, no, stop!" Connie shrieked frantically. "Oh! You cruel brute!... You'll kill her!"

I laughed. "Oh, no, Connie, she's all right—only a little erotic excitement!" I explained equably as I resumed the tickling, this time making Alice wriggle and scream in real earnest. She had not been allowed to satisfy her lustful cravings, induced by the sight of Connie's agonies, and by now she was in a terrible condition of fierce concupiscence and unsatisfied desires, dying to spend, but so far unable to do so for want of the spark necessary to provoke the discharge! More and more hysterical became Connie's prayers and pleadings, shriller her cries of genuine horror at the sight of Alice's cunt being so cruelly tickled—wilder and wilder became Alice's struggles and screams, till suddenly she shrieked, "For God's sake, make me spend!" Immediately I thrust the feather well up her cunt and rapidly twiddled it, then tickled her clitoris! A tremendous spasm shook Alice, her head fell back, then dropped on her bosom as she ejaculated: "A-h-h... ah-h-h!" in a tone of blessed relief, quivering deliciously as the rapturous spasm of the ecstasy thrilled through as she spent madly!

As soon as she came to herself again, I said to her, "Well, will you now yield yourself to me, or do you want some more?"

"Oh, no! No!—my God, no!" she cried, feigning to be completely subdued.

"You'll then be a good girl?"

"Yes!" she gasped.

"You'll do whatever I tell you to do?"

"Yes! Yes!" she cried.

"You'll let me... fuck you?"

"Oh, my God!..." she moaned, remaining silent. I touched her cunt with the feather. "Yes! Yes!" she screamed. "Yes!"

"That's right, dear!" I said encouragingly. Quickly I released her and put her into a large and comfortable easy chair in which she promptly coiled herself up, as if utterly exhausted and ashamed of her absolute surrender, but really to escape the sympathetic and pitying glances from Connie. It was as clever a piece of acting as I had ever seen!

I went across to Mrs. Blunt and without a word, I touched the springs and set the machinery at work. "Oh! Oh!" she cried as she felt herself drawn up again and her legs being remorselessly dragged asunder till she had resumed her late position. When I had her properly fixed, I said to her, "Now, Connie, I am going to punish you for abusing me. You'll have something to scream about!" I applied the feather to her lovely, but defenseless, cunt!

"Don't, don't!... Oh, my God!" she screamed. I saw we were about to have a glorious spectacle, so I stopped, blindfolded her, and beckoned to Fanny, who promptly came up, Alice also. Handing a feather to each, I pointed to Connie's quivering cunt.

Delightedly both girls applied their feathers to Connie's tender slit, Alice directing hers against Connie's clitoris, while Fanny ran hers all along the lips and as far inside as she could, their eyes sparkling with cruel glee as they watched Connie wriggle and listened to her terrible shrieks and hysterical ejaculations. It was a truly voluptuous sight! Connie naked, struggling frantically, while Alice and Fanny, also naked, were goading her into hysterics with their feathers! But soon I had to intervene. Connie by now was exhausted; she couldn't stand any more. Reluctantly, I stopped the girls, signaled to Fanny to disappear and Alice to return to her chair while I released Connie's bandage.

She looked at me seemingly, half-dazed, panting and gasping after her exertions.

"Now will you submit yourself to me, Connie?" I asked.

"Yes! Yes!" she gasped.

"Fucking and all!"

"Oh, my God!... Yes!"

I set her free. As she sank into her chair, Alice rushed to her as if impelled by irresistible sympathy. The two girls fell into each other's arms, kissing each other passionately, murmuring: "Oh, Connie!..."

"Oh, Alice!" The first part of the play was over!

THE SEA'S BARGAIN

by Michael M. Jones

The water closed in around her, crushing her under its immense weight, chasing away the light of the surface, dooming her to a dark, damp death where no one would ever find her. Her lungs screamed in protest, her body begged for oxygen, for a simple life-giving breath. She was lost, limbs flailing in a desperate attempt to find the surface, unable to figure out which way was up. Just...one...breath. The stale air pressed against her lips, forcing her to exhale. She opened her mouth, reflexes taking over, and the water flooded in. A deep, bone-rattling voice said from everywhere and nowhere.

Relax. Accept your fate. Embrace your destiny.

Naomi jerked awake, eyes flying open, gasping for breath that came easily and naturally. She gulped down the fresh, fan-cooled air of her apartment, and shook helplessly, curled in the middle of her bed. Just a dream. Just another damned dream. Except she knew what it meant. *Shit.*

Unable to sleep, she eventually got out of bed, and went to her computer. An hour later, all the necessary travel arrangements had been made.

Naomi jerked awake, eyes flying open, gasping for breath that came easily and naturally. She gulped down the fresh, fan-cooled air of her apartment, and shook helplessly, curled in the middle of her bed.

A month later, Naomi walked along the deserted shoreline of an island far, far from home. Well, it was far from where she lived. She couldn't forget that once upon a time, this had been her family's home, for untold generations before circumstances changed and necessity forced them to move on. It was a nameless speck on the map, a political oversight, the sort of thing everyone brushed under the rug and tried to make someone else's problem. Located deep in the Polynesian Triangle, somewhere between Hawaii and Samoa, it was remote, forgotten, and absolutely gorgeous. It was the sort of place a reality show might drop a bunch of quarreling, over-dramatic idiots, in order to make them perform tricks for their audience. Blue ocean, white sand, lush vegetation, a jungle wrapped around a long-dormant volcano – you expected to see the crew of the *Minnow* just around the next bend. Or maybe the skeletons of long lost British schoolboys.

Naomi amused herself with these thoughts while trudging barefoot through the sand, feeling its sun-baked warmth under her soles and between her toes. Fine sand, tiny seashells, and all the other debris of the tides, untouched by man for decades. It was hot out; she'd dressed for the occasion in denim shorts and a sky blue string bikini top which hugged her breasts quite nicely. She carried her sandals in one hand, and a drawstring bag over one shoulder. She'd left everything else back in the old village, which had stood up well under the passage of time and abandonment. *Almost*, she thought, *as if someone has been tending it all these years.* Not that she'd brought much with her. Either she wouldn't be here long, and wouldn't need it, or... she wouldn't need it at all. And wasn't that a cheerful thought.

Had someone seen her, they'd have known in a heartbeat that this was a true daughter of the island, come home at last. She was just into her 20's, of medium height, slim and athletic with the slender curves and well-honed muscles of a runner, small breasted and lithe. Her skin was bronze, her hair styled back in a long black braid, and her eyes a rich brown. Her features were strong, stubborn, and undeniably Polynesian, the family genes running strong despite generations of Americanization. An elaborate set of tattoos ran from her right shoulder down to just above the elbow. Sweeping lines, geometric symbols; and stylized creatures all combined to tell a larger story, one almost no one alive remembered in its entirety.

Though she'd never lived here, though she'd only visited the island once as a little girl, Naomi felt an undeniable welcome coming from all around her. Somehow, it didn't make her feel any better about the whole thing. She came to a halt, standing in the middle of the beach a thousand miles from anywhere, and turned to face the ocean. "We're really going to do this, aren't we," she said. It was neither question nor statement, but a resigned acknowledgment. "Fine. I'm here. You want me, come and get me."

A minute passed. Two. Three. Five. Ten. Naomi huffed and sat down where she was, feeling the warm sand under her bottom. Drawing her legs up to hug her knees with her looped arms, she stared out at the endless waves and the clear blue sky. "I'm not doing a song and dance," she said out loud, to the ocean. "You're not getting a ceremony out of me. I'm sorry, but that time is long past. I'm here because a deal was made a long time ago, and I'm too damned honorable or gullible to break it now. Even though I had no say in the matter. So here I am."

Still nothing. Naomi clambered to her feet. "Goddammit, you ancient oceanic asshole, if I came all this way for nothing, even after the nightmares... Do you even know what air travel is like these days? Of course not! So either you take me, or we call the whole thing off, and I'm going home," she yelled. "I had a perfectly nice life, you know, and – "

Slowly, ponderously, a gigantic tentacle broke the surface of the water, unfurling as it stretched high into the air. It paused, as if reaching for the sun, then slammed down onto the beach next to Naomi with a massive whomp! Sand billowed up from the impact, forcing her to shield her eyes until it settled. The tentacle was unbearably huge, taller than she was, longer than she could reasonably imagine, its sheer presence magnificent and terrifying. A second tentacle followed, rising out of the depths, slamming down on her other side. She was corralled, trapped in a cage of living flesh, surrounded by pulsing, razor-sharp suction cups. She was already starting to regret her words already.

"It's about time," she said instead, folding her arms. "So how does this work? Do you eat me whole, or tear me apart into little chunks, or am I slowly digested over a thousand years? I'd really appreciate it if you made this quick, but…I guess I understand if you want to make this last. You've been waiting for what, a hundred years? I bet the anticipation really gets to you after a while." She was babbling, and she couldn't help it.

The tentacles started to slide back into the ocean. One went directly. The other wrapped its very tip around her with surprising delicacy, like a gloved hand holding an egg. It plucked her from the sand, leaving behind her bag and sandals; before Naomi could say anything more, it dragged her underwater.

She was drowning. The endless water closed in all around her, the light of the sun quickly vanished, the murky blue depths became her entire world. The pressure increased as the tentacle dragged her further into what she expected to be a watery grave. Maybe it would let her pass out. Drowning wasn't the worst way to go, right? A minute passed, and her lungs strained, burning as they pleaded for oxygen. One breath and it would all be over….

The tentacles started to slide back into the ocean. One went directly. The other wrapped its very tip around her with surprising delicacy, like a gloved hand holding an egg. It plucked her from the sand, leaving behind her bag and sandals; before Naomi could say anything more, it dragged her underwater.

Quit struggling and relax. The voice was everywhere and nowhere, resonating in her head and in the water. *Just… breathe.* It was a voice she knew from her dreams.

She had no choice. The air burst from her parted lips. The water rushed in. She was drown – no, she was fine. She wasn't dying after all. She was breathing water. Impossible. *As impossible as the creature who's captured me?* she thought rebelliously. But how?

All will be explained.

"Ow! Knock it off with the Voice of God, there. It's giving me a headache!" she exclaimed. Rather, she tried to speak, but what came out were low, liquid syllables, carried through the water like a whale's song. Though the strange tones were unfamiliar, she understood their meaning in her heart.

We will soon converse properly. Relax.

What choice did Naomi have? She tossed caution to the currents, trying to relax. She breathed the water, boggling as her body adjusted to the lack of light, to the immense pressure, to the chill. Impossibly, she was alive well past the point of survival, seeing things that defied her imagination, things rarely seen by anyone. *I wish I had a camera for this.*

Time passed, impossible to track. Her movement slowed, finally halted. Oddly, there was light all around her, generated by a forest of luminescent sea plants dotting the ocean's floor in all directions. Strange fish swam in ever-changing schools, hideous creatures straight out of nightmare and gaudy things of brilliant colors and incredible hues. The tentacles released her, withdrawing into the blackness of an immense rocky cavern nearby, leaving Naomi drifting in a state of overwhelmed confusion. "Okay. So you prefer to eat at home. I get it. Who doesn't enjoy delivery now and again?"

I'm not going to eat you, Naomi.

She winced as once again, the omnipresent voice thundered inside her head. "Indoor voice?" she asked hopefully. "Please?"

There was a long sigh, like the ebbing of the tides. "You are a very strange person. Unlike any I've met before." Low, liquid syllables, just like her own speech had become, but she understood it. Male? Female? Impossible to tell. Curious, she moved/swam towards the cavern, despite every instinct screaming for her to get away. But then again, if the creature wanted her dead, it had had ample opportunity already.

There was a long sigh, like the ebbing of the tides. "You are a very strange person. Unlike any I've met before." Low, liquid syllables, just like her own speech had become, but she understood it. Male? Female? Impossible to tell. Curious.

There was movement within the cavern. The hint of something vast and unfathomable. Slithering tentacles. What might have been the blink of an eye the size of a football field. Light glinting across sharp, gigantic fangs.

Stop. The world-shaking tone was back; she hit it like a wall and came to a dead stop. *One moment.*

She waited. Things moved and slithered and crawled and twisted, the faint light unable to penetrate the cavern's depths enough to properly illuminate it. But then a person emerged. A woman. A gorgeous, naked, impossible woman.

She was tall and slender, streamlined with only a hint of curves. Her skin was iridescent and moon-pale, her eyes were huge and round and jet-black, her colorless hair streamed out behind her like froth on the waves. She looked delicate and fragile, yet something suggested incredible strength. Her features were inhuman and fey, carrying an alien otherness Naomi couldn't put into words. It was like looking in a funhouse mirror, everything stretched out and off-kilter, not knowing why you were so disturbed. Yet Naomi recognized a kind of beauty in the other woman. It called to her. Something within her answered. It stirred to life within her loins, a thread of desire uncoiling to fill her, warming her limbs and stroking her sex. She clenched her thighs together, trying to ignore the rising desire.

"What are *you*? Who are you?" she asked, staring at the woman. She suspected – no, she somehow *knew* that the creature in the cave was the woman before her.

"I have been called many things in my time," murmured the woman. "Beast, Devourer, Kraken, Ender-of-Things, Leviathan. Sulis, Amphitrite, Salacia. I have been feared and worshiped for as long as humans have dealt with the ocean." Her smile was slow and sly, showing off an array of razor-sharp teeth. Naomi shuddered, simultaneously attracted and repulsed by the sight. "Call me Hina. If you must call me anything at all."

"Hina." Naomi tried the name out. It fit. It frequently appeared in Polynesian myth. It meant "girl." Fitting yet utterly inappropriate. She liked it. "So you're a…goddess?"

"I am a child of the ocean. Fathered by the tides, mothered by the currents, born in storm and raised in darkness. Though I've been worshiped as a goddess, I'm more… primal. If it will help you wrap your mind around it, consider me a force of nature."

"Oh." Naomi's casual defiance had slipped away in the face of something so vastly different and more powerful. "So are you usually a tentacled horror from the deep?"

Hina laughed with genuine delight. "So forward! So bold! I must say, I really do like you, Naomi. It's such a lovely change of pace from those wanting to kill or appease me. You look me in the eye, and you treat me like you would anyone else. In a sense… yes. That is one of my forms. The oldest, most powerful, most feared. It is my birth form, the one I use to sink ships and destroy islands, to create tsunamis and devour whales. And yet, this is just as much me." She drew her hands down along the length of her naked, shimmering, humanoid form. She ran them over the barely-there breasts with their stiff nipples, and indicated her hairless sex with something like amusement. "Legs. Breasts. Cunt. Humans are *amazing*. So maybe it's not entirely accurate. I didn't really understand all the subtleties of the human form, and how they differed from the creatures of the sea. But it worked well enough whenever I took it to the surface for exploration and experimentation."

Exploration. Naomi gaped for a moment, trying to imagine the sort of things Hina might do on the surface. The things that came to mind – Hina writhing and moaning, wrapped around some fisherman, taking his cock into the sex she so clearly enjoyed, riding him until he collapsed – swept through her like a tidal wave. She shivered with unfulfilled need. "I – you know, your speech is very modern for a sea monster from beyond time."

Hina dismissed that with a wave of her hand. "It's all being filtered through your brain, darling. The same magic that lets you survive in my pocket of the ocean, that lets you breathe and talk, also lets you understand me in ways you'll find reassuring. I'm afraid that if we tried to communicate without it, your mind would shatter irrevocably under the ancient alien weight of my immortal consciousness. I hope you'll believe me when I say that I'd regret that. What you see here is as much a projection into your mind as it is real."

Hina dismissed that with a wave of her hand. "It's all being filtered through your brain, darling. The same magic that lets you survive in my pocket of the ocean, that lets you breathe and talk, also lets you understand me in ways you'll find reassuring.

"I'm sure. So why *am* I here, anyway? All I know is that centuries ago, my ancestors made some sort of deal with you. Survival or prosperity or calm seas, in exchange for the occasional sacrifice?"

"Oh, that."

"Oh, that? Yes, that." Naomi glared at Hina. "Go on."

Hina shrugged, a fluid movement involving her entire being. "As you might have figured out, I occasionally succumb to boredom or curiosity. Unlike many of my kind, I always found humans to be such strange, interesting, odd little things. Full of hopes and dreams and fears, with desires and appetites. In the old days, I went ashore frequently, and walked as a goddess. As times changed, that became less advisable. So I started making the odd deal here and there. Favors for companions, as it were. I'd ask for a virgin, or a first-born, or seven strapping young men, or the best hunter, or the cleverest maiden."

"Kind of like ordering the appetizer sampler?"

"Oh, sweetheart, I didn't *eat* them. I just wanted company. Someone interesting to talk to, and learn from." Hina sighed, and the ocean swelled around them. "I returned some when we were done. Others didn't want to go back. And some...just couldn't cope with the real me." She smiled, quick and sharp. "I'm a monster, not a *monster*. It's not my fault some brains are fragile." The look she then turned upon Naomi was almost sad. "I eventually stopped making deals altogether. People were less willing to negotiate with me. They wanted to hunt me, to document my existence, to dissect me. They wanted to quantify and qualify me. My time had passed. I retreated to my cave and for the most part, stayed there. You're here because your ancestor played the long game with me, convincing me to take the seventh daughter of the seventh generation. At the time, I was intrigued enough to let it happen. I thought it might be nice to have someone waiting for me that far down the road."

"My grandmother told me what little she knew of the story as it had been passed down," said Naomi after a moment of consideration. "All I knew is that I was of the right generation to be fed to a sea monster as part of an ancient bargain. And when I counted the women in my generation, and realized I was lucky number seven – well, I got the appropriate tattoos to signify it. I thought it was all myth and legend. Something to laugh at. Maybe something interesting to tell friends or lovers." She paused. "Until the dreams came, and I knew without a doubt where I had to go and what I had to do."

"Had you not upheld the bargain," said Hina, almost casually, "I'd have wreaked terrible vengeance upon you and yours, a thousandfold. I'd have shattered coastlines and drowned cities, and brought civilization crashing down into the deep blue sea. Perhaps I would have perished in the doing, for mankind is powerful and many and vindictive, but it would have been an apocalypse worth dying for." She gazed off into the distance, eyes wide, dark, and ancient. Naomi shuddered, hugging herself for the perception of warmth. "But!" announced Hina happily. "You came, and no one has to die after all. How wonderful!"

Naomi blinked, at a loss for words. There was something very unsettling about Hina's mood shifts and changeable demeanor. Just when you allowed yourself to relax... "So now what? Do we go back to your cave for drinks, while I explain the finale of The Sopranos to you, or something?" she asked nervously.

Hina took Naomi's hands in her own. Her skin was slippery and cool, more like a fish than a human; this close, Naomi could see the thin webbing between the fingers. "I had another idea," she murmured. "It's been a very long time since I've used this body. And a while since you've...enjoyed yourself. I saw it in your mind. I know you find me attractive. For what it's worth, I consider you to be a rather pleasing example of your kind also."

"I...er...thanks?" Naomi was pretty sure she'd just been complemented and propositioned. First time she'd ever been hit on by something older than civilization itself. It was...

"I...er...thanks?" Naomi was pretty sure she'd just been complemented and propositioned. First time she'd ever been hit on by something older than civilization itself. It was... flattering.

flattering. And far better than the drunken pickup lines she got at clubs all the time.

Hina kissed her with soft, warm lips. Without even thinking about it, Naomi returned the kiss. She was hesitant at first, but quickly forgot the weirdness factor, lost in the sensation. She'd been with her fair share of women, and Hina was by no means the worst kisser. There was a tentative playfulness, as the ancient creature re-accustomed herself to the pleasures of the flesh. Naomi soon took the lead, carefully guiding the kiss into something slow and deep, ever mindful of the sharp teeth and slightly alien feel of Hina's body against hers. There was definitely an art to it. *Actually*, Naomi's mind suggested, *the teeth kind of make it exciting*.

They broke the kiss after a few minutes, and Hina pulled back to study Naomi. "That was nice," she said. "I'm glad to see I'm not as out of practice as I'd feared."

"That was very nice," admitted Naomi, with a smile. "I really liked it." She reached out, running her fingertips over Hina's shimmering skin, growing used to the slippery coolness. Hina arched into the touch, proving that for all her oddities, she was a sensual creature. Naomi's hand drifted over one small breast, brushing the nipple, and Hina drew in a breath with a hiss of pleasure.

"I created this body to be...sensitive," she murmured. "I wanted the tactile experiences of the land. I'd forgotten just how sensitive it was." She tugged at Naomi's bikini top, pulling until it popped up to free her breasts as well. Naomi's nipples had already stiffened with arousal, reacting to the oddly erotic situation; the sudden feel of the ocean brushing over the now-bare skin momentarily unbalanced her. "Beautiful," said Hina, capturing a nipple between her fingers to give it a light tweak. "I really love the human form."

Naomi, caught off-guard as Hina pinched her nipple, moaned softly, before reaching out again to stroke her hands over the other woman's body. What followed was slow and lazy, a mutual exploration of hands and mouths sliding over flesh. Kissing, licking, teasing. Moaning, arching, gasping. They writhed together in the water with luxurious, deliberate movements, taking their measure of each other. Nails glided along backs and over buttocks, through hair and against sides. Hina delicately nipped at Naomi's tender skin with her sharp teeth, careful not to draw blood, and Naomi clenched inside with need every time. She was wet and hot, convinced she'd birth an underwater volcano from her slow-burning lust. She wriggled free of her shorts and bikini bottoms, utterly naked, giving herself to the ocean.

When Hina slipped her fingers into Naomi's sex, it was with ease, she was so wet and ready. Three elegantly long fingers curled within her, fluttering and stroking, teasing her clit, pressing her buttons, filling her, pushing her. Naomi thrust against the hand, insistent and wanton, every movement sending a little wave against her core; when she came, it was an explosion like she'd never felt. The storm caught her, swept her up, threw her around, dropped her back into Hina's arms, gasping and panting and cross-eyed. She managed to focus, finding something naked and vulnerable in the immortal creature's own eyes. She kissed Hina before slipping her hand between the woman's legs to explore her hairless sex. Despite the coolness of her skin, Hina was blazing hot inside, soaked with arousal. She tense, tight and demanding, around

When they'd both recovered from the initial round of exploration, Naomi slid down to taste Hina, thoroughly curious. She tasted like the ocean's very essence: salty and wild, uncontrollable, unfathomable, deep. Like the ocean intensified to its utmost self. Naomi drove her tongue deep into Hina's sex, lapping and licking, before shifting to suck at her clit.

Naomi's questing hand, riding her with enthusiasm and need. She pressed herself to Naomi, rocking back and forth with ever-increasing speed until she came. Far, far above them, the waves swelled and crashed, slamming down on beaches for hundreds of miles in every direction.

When they'd both recovered from the initial round of exploration, Naomi slid down to taste Hina, thoroughly curious. She tasted like the ocean's very essence: salty and wild, uncontrollable, unfathomable, deep. Like the ocean intensified to its utmost self. Naomi drove her tongue deep into Hina's sex, lapping and licking, before shifting to suck at her clit. As the ancient sea goddess wailed her pleasure, Naomi felt something sliding between her legs. Neither tongue nor fingers, but shaped just right and surprisingly versatile. It filled her, pulsing and shifting deep within. A dozen tiny mouths kissed the inside of her pussy, sucking and teasing; Naomi about screamed as the sensations overwhelmed her. She channeled it all into taking her fill of Hina. The orgasms ripped through them both simultaneously, crashing like a tsunami.

Naomi didn't want to know what had just happened, but she knew she liked it. *This explains so much hentai*, she thought much later, when she had cause to consider it. *Who knew?*

Ultimately, all good things had to come to an end. Exhausted, the two women curled together on the ocean floor, a satiated Hina draped over the still bemused Naomi. "I thought *I* was supposed to eat *you*," Hina said with a low, tired chuckle.

"I guess we got things backwards," replied Naomi. "Not that I'm complaining." She nestled against Hina, and her eyes slowly closed, dropping her into a deep, dreamless sleep.

Bargain satisfied.

"But..." She protested, somewhere deep in the back of her mind.

It would be cruel to keep you here. A tentacle wrapped around her, gently, lovingly. It lifted her.

"What if I want to stay?"

You would grow restless. Unhappy. Homesick. This is for the best. Up she went, rising through the water.

"I'll miss you."

Come back in a year. She was deposited back on the beach, as carefully as a father putting a baby to sleep.

"It's a promise."

When she woke up, she was lying on the beach, fully dressed and thoroughly rested. There was no sign that anything had ever happened. But she knew without a doubt she'd come home again next year.

Michael M. Jones is a writer, editor, and book reviewer. He's appeared in numerous anthologies from Circlet Press and Cleis, including Lustfully Ever After, She-Shifters, *and* Seductress. *He lives in Southwest VA with just enough books, a pride of cats, and a wife who loves the sea. Visit him at www.michaelmjones.com.*

EVERYTHING OLD IS NEW AGAIN II

322

SERIE 75

10

3512

10

SERIE 55

MISS SWEDISH EROTICA

by Seka

"The Platinum Princess" look, from "Inside Seka", 1981.

There were loops and there were features. Only the biggest stars got to do features. On the other hand, there were a lot more loops being done than features, so lots of A-List porn stars did loops as well, in between features. The whole thing was like baseball. You began in the rookie leagues, then moved up to the minor leagues, and finally the majors – except even those in the majors still played in the high minors now and then just to make ends meet.

Loops were often compiled together into a sort of feature, kind of like a mix tape. For that reason, the same scene might be used not only in one compilation, but in any number of compilations. That's why it's a joke when porn actors try to count how many movies they've been in. You do one scene and it ends up in twenty different compilations. Is that one film or twenty? Worse yet, we never got paid for the multiple times a scene was used. We'd get paid for a day's work and that was it. Sometimes we'd complain and get suckered into making a deal for "something on the back end," which was a total joke. We'd be promised some sort of percentage or something down the line, but none of us ever saw a dime. We got what we got paid for that one day's work and not a penny more, even if that scene was used a million times, forever and ever, amen.

The top name in loops was Swedish Erotica. They were the big time, the place where even the features actors continued to work even after they'd become big stars.

The top name in loops was Swedish Erotica. They were the big time, the place where even the features actors continued to work even after they'd become big stars.

Soon Swedish Erotica came calling for me, and I completely flipped out. Unlike most new girls who came on the adult scene, my time spent working in Ken's stores taught me who was who in the business. When I went to meet with them I thought, "Damn, I can really make a living at this. If these guys are here, I've arrived."

We met, we hit it off, and I was the new Swedish Erotica Girl. Of course, there were a lot of Swedish Erotica girls, but now I was part of their stable of players. Their loops were probably the most popular in the adult book stores, and their compilations were spliced together and ran as if they were features in adult movie theaters – a thing of the past from back in the days before home video. And once home video came around, their compilation tapes were always top sellers – not that I saw any financial benefit.

I was doing scenes constantly. It all became more comfortable and natural for me. I began to see some of the same faces both in front of and behind the camera, which made me less apprehensive when I'd show up for a day at work. And it was work. For a twenty-minute scene, I'd be there all day long, doing this, doing that. Waiting, lots of waiting, just like in a mainstream movie.

Whenever I walked into a room, all eyes were on me. This crazy, accidental look of mine was turning heads. It made me very self-conscious, but I used that to my advantage. Do I shock you? Good. It puts you on your heels and me in a position of strength. I became less and less of a wallflower. I wouldn't call myself a diva, but if something was way out of line, I wasn't afraid to say so – politely and professionally – and it usually got fixed. The bedspread was dirty – get me a clean one. I needed a cigarette break – I asked and I got one. Pretty basic stuff that professional, polite parties should be able to work out without a big fuss, which was not always the case between filmmakers and actors. Some of the girls were treated like meat and it continued because they accepted it. I didn't. I liked the money I was making and the attention I was being given, but I wasn't really thinking long term. It was good for now, but if they fired me, I'd do something else tomorrow. It never occurred to me that if I pissed someone off I'd be lying in a gutter, begging for spare change. I always seemed able to bounce from one thing to another. I may not have been a career girl in the classic sense, but that actually worked to my advantage. Someone who wanted to be an accountant would be more worried that if they had a blow-out with a boss they'd not only lose their job, they might never work as an accountant again. Me, I had no problem changing what I wrote on an application when it asked for "occupation." I was whatever I was doing at that moment. Work of some kind was everywhere for a person willing to do it.

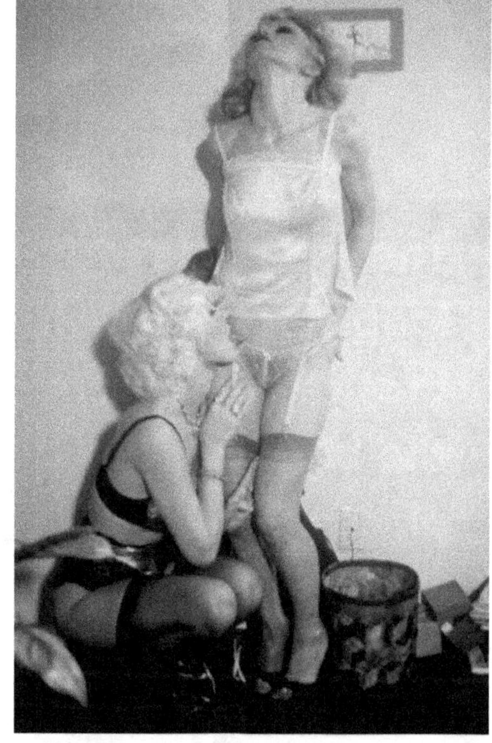
A little girl/girl action with Merle Michaels.

Swedish Erotica had a certain image. For whatever reason, they wanted the girls in their scenes to wear lacy scarves. It was weird, but as it was explained to me, they wanted customers to see that scarf in a scene and make an immediate association in their head, "Oh, a scarf. This is Swedish Erotica." It was like a hood ornament on a car: every car had its own design and it helped you know what kind of car it was.

Swedish Erotica thought that scarves were classy. I thought they were itchy and a pain in the ass to wear. I mean, in real life, who wears a scarf to bed? I can see keeping some article of clothing on – usually sweat socks. Ha! But even to be sexy, there are a lot cooler things to wear, like silky lingerie. But that was their signature and for as much as I asked for things here and there, removing the scarf was one thing on which they would not negotiate.

The more loops I did for Swedish Erotica, the more I became personally associated with scarves. People started to forget all the other girls in their loops who wore them, too. But I was doing so many scenes for them, I started being known in the industry and even among the fans as Miss Swedish Erotica. At one point, Swedish Erotica even gave me that title officially, like it was an-

But the scarves – those damn scarves. I hated them. You'd go to a shoot and they'd have them lying around everywhere and would just throw one at me or the other girls.

other beauty contest I had won. It was all good. They'd invite me to public appearances and things and introduce me as Miss Swedish Erotica, just like when I was Miss Hopewell Virginia. I don't know how they came up with it. I don't believe there was any official voting of any sort. It was a publicity stunt, which flattered me because they were saying, essentially, that I was now the face of their franchise. I was moving up in the world.

But the scarves – those damn scarves. I hated them. You'd go to a shoot and they'd have them lying around everywhere and would just throw one at me or the other girls. They'd been lying on the floor – dirty, dusty, covered in cum and whatever. They made me want to retch. As soon as I was handed one, I'd go to the bathroom and hand-wash it, then blow it dry before I'd let it touch my skin; otherwise I thought I was going to pick up some kind of disease. It was like being asked to wear someone else's skanky underwear that was just fished out of a dumpster. They never washed those things on their own. It wasn't like they were fancy or expensive or anything. For a buck or two they could have given us brand new ones for every scene; but no, they recycled them. Makeup, sweat, and cum, lots of dried cum. Maybe it was more noticeable when I wore one in a scene because mine were nice and clean and fluffy. I can be pretty anal sometimes. I may have been raised poor, but we were always big on cleanliness.

One time I was doing a phone-in radio appearance. I put my phone on speaker and started doing housework. When the station called, the first thing they asked me on the air was, "So, Seka, what are you doing right now," expecting some sort of sexy answer. I, being slow on the uptake, opted for honesty. "I'm steam-cleaning my toilet right now." They laughed hysterically and thought I was being funny. I wasn't. Steam-cleaning toilets and hand-washing scarves: that's how I roll.

People were recognizing the platinum blonde from all the scenes I was doing, but especially the Swedish Erotica ones wearing the scarf. Even once I moved up to features, I continued to do Swedish Erotica scenes, except now I was doing them with all the top stars. I became the franchise. And as for the scarves? As time went by, I started to get fan mail and stuff and realized how much the scarves stayed in people's minds, so I began packing mine away after I'd used one. Those things are worth a pretty penny to fans today, and I've still got some.

This has been an excerpt from Inside Seka, *available from Bearmanor Media (www.bearmanormedia.com) or through Amazon.com.*

PORN KING

by John Holmes

Above the Sunset Strip in the Hollywood Hills, a new club had opened. Its name was Eden and it catered exclusively to couples and single women. Open only on weekends, Eden was an immediate sensation, often turning away as many as 2,000 customers a night. "You're a big reason for my success," the owner, a former cop, excitedly confided to me one evening. "You're the draw. People want to see you and meet you."

I didn't want to get caught up in the night club scene again when I was first asked to attend. I was filming, putting in long hours virtually each day of the week. But my weekends were free and I couldn't stay away. My inquisitive mind got the best of me, and I quickly became a regular.

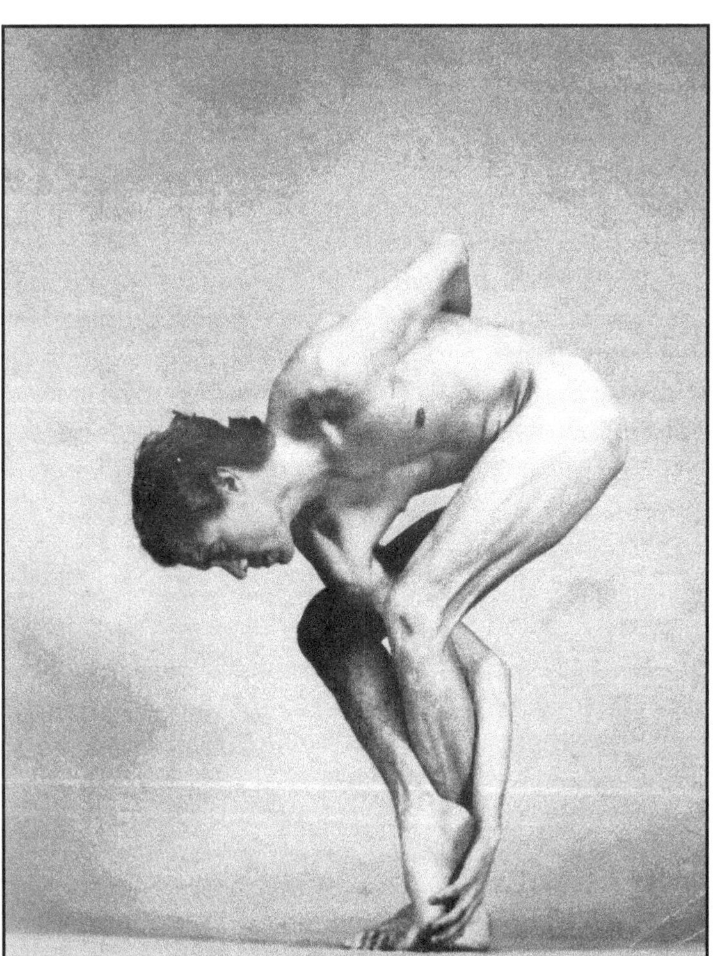

The action at Eden was frantic. People somehow found their way there from all parts of the country to be a part of the "swinging singles" experience that was sweeping America. Eden was swinging, to be certain, everything from singular groping and nudity to group sex. I met some fascinating people, among them a couple who offered me ten thousand dollars to father a child for them, a request I turned down.

Bored with the teeming activity, I began to stray from Eden to begin a series of relationships, fancying myself a romantic.

I was first smitten with an actress who was then with a well-known pop singer. When those pairings failed I began seeing a real knockout lady with a sensational body. A dancer, she had starred in films and was currently headlining in Las Vegas. She was also unhappily married. For that reason we agreed never to have intimacies at her house, only at the apartment she had leased for me. Six months into our relationship, she invited me to her home. It was safe, she told me; her husband was away on business. Besides, we'd been drinking and everything was fine with the world.

John and Ginger, *Girls on Fire.*

My leggy friend and I were in bed were in bed when we heard a sound at the front door. Jumping from her arms stone naked, I grabbed my clothes and ran for the sliding glass door that led to the terrace. Outside in the darkness, as I began to step into my pants, I heard gunfire. Then I felt the searing pain in my leg. The force of the blow hurdled me over the terrace rail and down the ivy-covered hillside. Still naked but now bloodied and in pain, I somehow managed to climb back up the slope to my car and drive to the nearest hospital, where I passed out on the steering wheel horn.

When I woke up I was facing two uniformed policemen who were full of questions about the gunshot wound. I was quiet for along moment as I strained to come up with a possible alibi. Nothing made sense so I said with all the sincerity I could muster, "I'm a stunt man in the movies. I was rehearsing for a scene when my prop gun went off. I didn't know it was real."

Between all my running around and whoring, I had made a handful of feature films myself. The names of the earliest ones are long forgotten, but I believe *The Ladies Bed Companion* was among the first.

The cops looked at each other, shaking their heads. I'm sunk, I told myself. Then one of the men said, "Stupid. Be more careful next time."

"You're right," I answered. "And I will."

With that, they were gone.

I let out a sigh of relief and began to relax. No more encounters with the police, I vowed silently. No more! I wanted to take my vow seriously, but somehow I couldn't. There was no way of predicting what the future held for me. I couldn't even predict what tomorrow would bring. Not so surprisingly, perhaps, my dancer friend continued to remain in my life. Or, rather, I continued to remain in hers when she divorced her husband and moved me into her house. Being a dancer, she knew all about legs. I couldn't have had a better therapist to get me back on my feet.

The relationship held yet another surprise for me, however. After nearly a year together she let one of her dainty shoes drop. She had secretly remarried and was supporting her new husband in Las Vegas. How was I to know she was seeing another man during her frequent trips away for headlining performances? It was time for me to move on.

More despondent than I cared to admit over the breakup, I became a regular at the bars of Beverly Hills' posh hotels where I became chummy with the bartenders. "You get a lot of lonely, rich old ladies looking for some action," I told them. "*I'm* the action. Fix me up and I'll cut you in on the take." I met some fascinating ladies and received the usual expensive gifts, including complimentary "vacations" for two to such destinations as London, Paris and Rome, but I was like dead meat on the rack. I had lost all enthusiasm for what I was doing. I was smoking and drinking more than ever,

The sexual revolution was reaching an all-time high. Within the Los Angeles area, a number of individuals were beginning to organize companies and invest huge amounts of money in making adult entertainment. Theaters were opening in major cities for the exclusive showing of porno movies. Following the release of such films as *Deep Throat* and *The Devil in Miss Jones*, branded obscene but upheld by the courts, the public no longer seemed to have a problem with being seen in lines at porno movie houses. Unlike the days of seedy-looking men with long trench coats, it had actually become acceptable for couples, even groups of friends, to attend such places. Porn had suddenly become a part of popular culture.

Between all my running around and whoring, I had made a handful of feature films myself. The names of the earliest ones are long forgotten, but I believe *The Ladies Bed Companion* was among the first.

Feature movies were definitely a step above loop life. Scripts weren't necessary to churn out a loop, and besides, scripts were evidence if found in a raid. Now we were given actual pages with storylines and dialogue to memorize. And we had shooting schedules of days instead of hours.

I had met Hawaiian-born director Bob Chinn in 1970. Now, several years later, I ran into him again. "I'm making another porn flick," Chinn told me," and I'd love for you to be in it." What Bob had in mind, I didn't know, but he certainly came along at the

While in Hawaii for *Waikiki Wadd*, I signed a contract to work nights at a dingy downtown Honolulu club performing simulated sex on stage with an attractive young partner. We never did anything but we were nude and the act was choreographed to such a point that it was highly erotic. The girl and I created such a sensation that the club owner kept renewing our options.

right time.

The chance encounter led to my being cast as Johnny Wadd, a no-nonsense, gun-toting private eye à la Dirty Harry, whose capers led him into more beds than dark alleys. At first, Chinn had no name for his character. We were standing around MacArthur Park in Los Angeles one afternoon when he asked me if I had any ideas what to call the film. "Why not name the lead guy Johnny Wadd," I suggested, "and that could be the title of the film." Being of Chinese descent, Bob didn't immediately understand what "Johnny Wadd" implied, but after trying it out on a few people he got the message and decided to use it.

Johnny Wadd was my first real screen characterization and *Johhny Wadd, Detective*, my first film with Bob Chinn, was a great working experience for me. It had a plot with substance, a large cast and crew, a six-week shooting schedule, a big budget, and location filming. For the first time I had a chance to work away from sheltered studio walls.

Bob and I made a good team. He allowed me to shape my character, whose trademarks were a big dick and a pinkie ring (an enormous diamond-encrusted dragonfly that had been given to me by a lady friend as a reward for "services rendered"), as well as giving me free reign in the creation of my sex scenes. I didn't tell Bob how to edit and he didn't tell me how to fuck.

Following *Johnny Wadd, Detective*, we made *Ensenada Wadd* on location in Mexico. Filming on location has its drawbacks, as we soon discovered. While in Ensenada to shoot prison conditions and squalid street scenes for background shots, we were threatened with arrest for working without a permit. Facing a possible five-year jail sentence, we were able to escape only because our newer, revved-up engines could outrun the posse.

While in Hawaii for *Waikiki Wadd*, I signed a contract to work nights at a dingy downtown Honolulu club performing simulated sex on stage with an attractive young partner. We never did anything but we were nude and the act was choreographed to such a point that it was highly erotic. The girl and I created such a sensation that the club owner kept renewing our options.

The act continued long after the completion of *Waikiki Wadd.* In fact, months passed before I had to return to Hollywood for the start of another film. I gave the club owner two weeks' notice, but he would not let me go. The next thing I knew, I was being arrested on lewd conduct charges and heading for a trial which lasted five months. It seemed odd to me that while I was free on bail I was allowed to continue performing at the club. It seemed less odd when I realized that I had been set up by the club owner. With one phone call to a friend at the police department, he got what he wanted: more of me and a lot of free publicity.

Johnny Wadd pushed me into the limelight. I had more offers to appear in films than I could handle, and that wasn't all. I was wanted for personal appearances at various Miss Nude USA contests, film premieres, and trade shows, as well as for numerous endorsements and magazine interviews. Whenever I showed up at a public event the atmosphere was like a carnival. People were lined up around the block to get my au-

tograph. Men asked me to deflower their daughters. "How big is it?" Fans would scream.

"Bigger than a pay phone, smaller than a Cadillac," was my stock reply.

I was traveling all over the world with all expenses paid and making thousands of dollars just to sign my name and promote movies. The women in other parts of the world were just as hot, if not hotter, than the women in America.

I had become the biggest name in adult films; the highest paid performer in the industry. The John Wayne of pornography! And I was working my ass off, often in risky situations. One producer got me stranded in the dead of night in a remote California desert. There I was, fighting off million of ants and bees, without any clothes on. Then there was the time a knife-wielding leading lady took the director literally when he yelled, "Cut!" I've been filmed having sex atop rocky ledges, rooftops, pianos, the hoods of cars, and a Paris Metro platform, aboard airplanes, boats, trains, and helicopters, and, of all places, at the corner of Hollywood and Vine. I love to work in bed, but I've gone through phases where they've put me in the most insane settings. That makes it more exciting for everyone, I suppose, except for the person who has to make it happen.

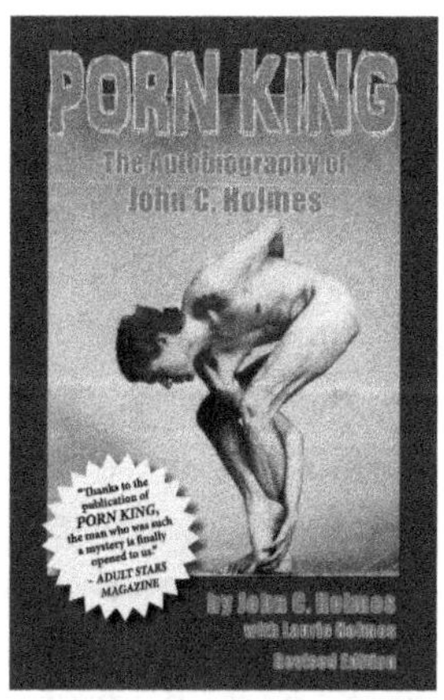

This has been an excerpt from Porn King: The Autobiography of John C. Holmes, *available from Bearmanor Media (www.bearmanormedia.com) or through Amazon.com.*

huts for the fantasy inclined. The décor, simple and fur-lined. A round room of exquisite, slightly demur Aureolin beauty. There was no one else playing anything at the moment, and none of the puzzles on the clean triangle tables were more than 10% done. Janie merely stood, undecided.

"Drink?" Maugham offered.

"What've you got?" asked the father.

"Oh, it can all be accomplished."

"Diet A&W?" asked the mother.

The hostess smiled as if knowing she'd won. "All" was always a challenge, but at these prices, Maugham could afford to stock everything cold that was in popular culture.

The father added, "I'll have bourbon and Mountain Dew."

"You will," Maugham agreed. In a moment she was passing liquids like favors, sitting, smiling, hand on her button, hidden by a big blue desk.

"We received your kind donation," Maugham droned. "Thank you. Kind you. We'd like to do your little girl a favor." She winked. "We go through the motions because we are a non-profit, and short-sighted Minnesota men are only keeping us from advertising on *giant* billboards."

"Uh..."

"Dad! Dad. I know." Maugham held up some hand. "Down to the gristle. You're in agreement with terms?"

Nods all around.

Music began: steamy, sweaty sax. Maugham finished her gulp of ice water and Mandarin Cosmopolitan and asked, "Are you wanting to accomplish anything specific?"

The father said, "I think – "

"Besides the obvious. For instance – and I don't mean this as crass as it is but – are you wanting her steeped in technique? A fun plus time? Is it a sort of graduation present?" When no response offered itself: "Are you seeking a certain theme? Superman or werewolf, for instance. We are fully adaptable with costumes. Rather than picking from a list, limit your imagination to naught and let *her* have fun with it." A pause. "A warden, perhaps. A forest ranger – during a fire – I like that one. In theory. A pop star. Or *she* could be any of these. A hairy bear. A computer programmer. A pheasant plucker's mate. A zoo official."

"Just fuck her," the father said casually. His drink wasn't working yet.

"Agreed," said the hostess.

A button must have been pushed. A heavy, manly door opened and in walked a young man of 20, shaven, smelling of man perfume, adequately attired somewhere between spiffy and comfortable, hands clasped in front.

"This is the gentleman who will be fucking your daughter. Lyi."

"Hello," said Lyi.

Leaning forward slightly, Maugham asked the mother, "Would you like him to wear glasses?"

Mother looked at father and they nodded. "Yeah, that would be nice."

"Would it? Lyi."

At which point Lyi removed his actual glasses from his inside shirt pocket and stood there as one does when being talked about up close.

"We won't *draw* this out," said Maugham, "but psychologically, how do you want little Janie fucked?"

She fretted over what position to assume. If he entered her. Should she be on her side, hand on chin, hand wistfully playing with pubes? Though she didn't know they were called pubes.

In the plight of uncertainty, feeling the effects of the Mt. Dew, the father said his one word: "Well…"

"Lyi."

To which Lyi took his cue and recited his business. "Do you want her to know ecstasy; do you want her to cum? Or do you just want hymen broken? Are you giving her the most exciting night of her life, is this a graduation present? Or would you like a date night, with full conversation and flowers?"

Maugham opened the flower book on her desk and said, "Details we'll leave to Lyi, but these are isolated examples to act upon."

The parents looked at each other, uncertain as Christmas presents.

"Last questions. Promise."

The room was a dark box that stood eight feet tall and smelled of lilies. New age piano, instrumentals – the girl's choice – intruded ominously, softly from all sides as Janie laid naked on the bed. Arms outstretched, legs and toes stretched, she couldn't touch the edges of the bed. It was just that big. The only thing she'd been told was to *make yourself comfortable*. Nudity seemed required.

But it was taking longer than she expected. There was nothing to read in the room. No television. It was boring. And bothersome.

She fretted over what position to assume. If he entered her. Should she be on her side, hand on chin, hand wistfully playing with pubes? Though she didn't know they were called pubes. Perhaps the bolder, legs spread, pussy pointed at the door like a weapon of singular destruction. Maybe already moaning, squeezing her tits, playing with wherever it was that brought pleasure to a girl? She'd seen *The Sweetest Thing*, and that was porn, but it didn't set any clear guidelines.

And what to say? Open with something cool. Yes. She had a dictionary of quotes at home, but she hadn't cracked that since her *Roughing It* book report.

The door opened slowly. Spooked proper, Janie rushed through the sexy and practical choices, confusing and combining them into nothing, culminating in her head being raised slightly above the duck down pillow, hands hiding the good stuff, though not from habit.

"Hey," Lyi said. He stood with a chilling coolness. His hazel eyes sparked like solar paneling and his teeth sparkled gingerly as if the toothpaste still worked.

In deference to "hey" Janie held up a hand briefly for introductions and let it slowly fall back across a tit. Her other hand instinctively clutched the rose-colored bedsheets as *the boy* moved further into the room.

If he wasn't circling her, then he was smiling. Trying an eye that said *I am fruity, I am safe sin, come on, girls*. He had a mouth that knew things.

"My name's Lyi." And he undulated his jacket.

Janie forgot her name, but it didn't matter. Lyi unbuttoned his sleeve, saying, "Relax. This is good." The other sleeve's buttons were undone and somehow that calmed her. "What I want to know is..." He jumped on the bed. "Why are you naked?"

He smiled at her. She, trembling. Stomach, knotting and knowing it had to recite Shakespeare it didn't know. Like that time –

"Are you with me?" he asked, suddenly, marveling her body. She shook, shaking her head. He put a hand on a hand that was hiding nipple. "Then get dressed," he whispered.

Crawling off the bed, she brushed her ears long enough to ask, "Are they watching us?"

"There's nobody else here, sweetheart," he purred manly.

"I don't really want you to fuck me." Clothes went on. She sprayed perfume on her tits before crawling into her top, because it was there and, she assumed, free.

"Oh, are you into carpet?"

She crossed her eyes and answered hesitantly, "I like carpet; yeah."

Relief came to the boy. He updid his pants buttons, saying, "That's fine! Parents don't get it. Do they? On the ground floor you can get that. Just tell Maugham and she'll assign you."

"What do you mean?" She looked at him, tits pointing through her shirt. "Carpet? What do I want – "

"Okay, yeah, okay, that's all right." He was near. His hand on her shoulder now. She sweated, waiting, waiting for rape. "This isn't about floor coverings. You like girls, don't you?"

Fear was hers. Tangled her in its crappy, crass emotions and left her with little to think with. Lyi noticed that the little red spots she carried weren't confined to her face, blotching her complexion like a redhead. Which she didn't seem to be. A quick beaver recon proved her silky blonde, so perhaps she was partial to chocolate or unfavorable skin heredity.

Her nose, he noticed, hooked like Donna Lewis, but without the singer's fortune with round cheeks and delectable eyes. (Eyes that could cry.) Her lips were full like diapers and she had a large brown mole between her nose and where the ghost of a mustache challenged her smile. The acne wasn't severe, but it infiltrated even her pen-thin eyebrows and even into the inner skin of her nose so that, a few times a minute, she squeezed it as a scratch. Like Christina Ricci, she had too much forehead and a used mop of semi-blonde hair pulled back into an unclasped ponytail. And her eyes, he thought, were ever so slightly cross-eyed, like that Japanese skater Mao, and those grayish circles that contained her eyes could have been spaced better.

In the moment this rating occurred Janie was struggling with how much to say. She doubted all the way here that any amount of pleading would keep her from getting fucked.

But she knew she had to try. Besides, Lyi *looked* normal. Not at all the 50-year-old zit she'd expected. And nice. And clean, and he *listened.*

"I like boys..."

"Just not me," but he smiled and flopped on the bed. "It's okay, you know."

"What is?"

"Whatever you want," he said to the ceiling, covered with giant tattoos. "Any *time*, any distance. *You* make the moves. Or I take myself out of the game. You can have an Italian or something."

"Like a sub? A sausage?"

He laughed, above her, not at her. Suddenly the room had room, and comfort.

She could touch him now. It was bearable. Her hand just fit his arm.

"Maybe I'm not your type, I meant." He said it softly, like night FM radio. Using his face muscles and the subtleties of smile, Lyi bounced off the bed and walked around in model fashion. "Blondes, brunettes, there are all kinds of builds. What's your ideal guy?"

He was pleasant to watch – like the news. Comfortable, kinda.

After thought – the thought that spilled out the hours of thought she'd spent before on the subject – she replied, "You're fine. You're very man like."

"Thanks." He sat on the bed, and tapped the empty space for her ass. As she slowly scooted, he said, "You don't have to do anything. We can talk."

"My parents thought I should get fucked," she said without blinking. "They could fuck themselves."

"They could." He thought. "Maybe they should."

"My *guy* should be everything. I guess. Everything."

"So he should *get* everything."

She put a hand on his hand. Understanding purchased much. Close, she thought, and squeezed his third finger, and fully opened up. "I was looking up hymen on Health and I'd really – "

"On the net."

"On the net," she nodded and squeezed the hair of his backhand, "I want to *give* him myself. Just like he should me. That's all I mean."

Lyi was staring at the floor. "I know, Janie. It's important to you. That's easy. We don't have to *do* anything."

She sighed, smiled. Thanked him by gripping more hairs. He patted her hand. Smooth hand, but for the pimple.

She put a hand on his hand. Understanding purchased much. Close, she thought, and squeezed his third finger, and fully opened up. "I was looking up hymen on Health and I'd really – "

"You want to watch something?"

She nodded.

"It's all porn, I'm afraid."

"Oh."

He went to rifle the stash – no DVD cases, merely sleeved French and Euro titles. "But some of the Laure Sainclair is very story-oriented. Actually, the acting's good. Why they dub themselves in their own language, I don't know."

Masquerade chosen, the kids settled against the very back of the bed, too far away to see the 26" TV *clearly*, and watched French people commence fiction. As Lyi remoted the speed to 20x through the credits, a greater comfort settled over Janie, like blanket on top of blanket. Three blankets under, just before the widow's scene, she spoke.

"Won't you get in trouble for this?"

"Nah. Did you parents drop you?"

"They're probably downstairs," she said. "We didn't talk about pickup."

"Maybe we should sound a couple of these through then, for the sound."

He raised the sounds of Laure's fucking dubs. Her, pounded in the ass by perhaps a grieving friend of the family. It was the first Europorn Janie had ever seen.

"You think they're listening?" she asked loudly. The question had hung on her tongue ever so slightly. She was intrigued by Laure's perfect ass going at regular speed, twat on the floor. *Did that hurt?*

"No," Lyi said. "Definitely."

Definitely listening or definitely not? It didn't explain why they, *us*, were listening to this, watching this…stuff.

For the sound. She remembered.

Something was stirring. Within her. Somewhere. Laura's pounding moans were gloriously loud.

"Sometimes," the boy continued, "I accept gratuities for doing this. But I never get in trouble."

"That's… like tips. For what?"

"Not hitting it. Sometimes a girl is just so frightened, frightened to death. Because you're in another country almost. You have respect the fear. No one should have to deal with *raw fear* unless you're trapped in a place. Like *Predators*, in a jungle, or your car is going over the bridge. You're not *trapped* here, Janie. This isn't life and death."

"Thanks." A few minutes into the next fuck, she said, "I'd like to do that. You've been really nice. I've…"

From a Hello Kitty billfold she removed two twenties. There were smaller bills in there, but except for the odd waiter and doorman, her tipping skills on giving money to strangers for not doing something to her was less than limited. It seemed the right amount.

From a Hello Kitty billfold she removed two twenties. There were smaller bills in there, but except for the odd waiter and doorman, her tipping skills on giving money to strangers for not doing something to her was less than limited. It seemed the right amount.

The boy took it without a struggle. Hardly with a glance. "Thanks. I'm taking this because you wouldn't believe what they pay here."

You're a whore? she wanted to ask. But after the giving of money it seemed wholly rude.

"Don't worry, they won't find out from me," he said kindly, watching a game Czech take it up the ass.

"Thanks."

There didn't seem to be anything else to say. Lyi had skipped forward a couple scenes, to Laure playing with her French pastry. He turned up her noise louder. Janie closed her eyes, and in time, inched her hand to find his.

"Do you mind if I jack?"

"What's that?"

"Play with myself."

Eww was her thought. She'd caught her father at it, just once, while he chewed Big Red. It was a disgusting flashback. She kept Lyi's hand in hers. He started some up and down with his left hand, but she didn't look.

Lyi laughed and said, "I'm kidding." Though he wasn't.

After an hour, they thought it was safe. Her parents had asked for the pleasant approach anyway, so just waiting 15 or 10 minutes wouldn't do. Now they felt time had pressed on long and pro enough. Both non-sexual partners left the fuck chamber, a little unsure of step, straightening a little clothes. Janie held her shoes in her hand.

From the railing on the stairs, she looked up into the endless ceiling. Lyi had told her a little history of the place while they waited it out. The brownstone, affectionately known by the "inmates" as Whitehall, because of its intense darkness, was erected in 1923 by an aging Madame of petite proportions who installed local girls into the place and took no more than 20% in cash from whatever it was they did in the rooms. Madame neither knew nor cared. She had learned to be clean of conscious from all the raids she'd lived through in Arizona. Through the years the structure retained his sexual nature, drifting into various states of brothel, until Domin Maugham, an unemployed children's book illustrator, discovered a sexual loophole in supply and demand. No one was fucking the ugly people. When Stan Friedberg, a passing acquaintance and previous brothel keeper, was putting the old place up for sale, Maugham rallied around the banks, lying to all about what she wanted the money for, and caught enough cash to allow her to *just* beat out the others at the estate auction. Through months of not really struggling – there are so many uglies out there, she thought, and was proven right – she paid off the mortgage in full, and was now in charge of a trend setter. Out West there were high-falutin' Ugly Fuckers (you can't copyright an idea) springing up, but Maugham could safely, proudly say that she owned the original.

Janie's parents, who had little interest in their own private parts these days, and so would not partake of the "parents' freebie" that had been offered, had been enclosed in the Trad room. There they were treated to a variety of CNN channels. The taut taupe sofa was comfy, and their offered coffee had steamed.

With a knock and not waiting for a response Janie stepped into the room and tried to glow. Only the braces on her teeth did this. But it was enough that she'd loosened a smile, a rare thing in her teen life.

Dad was quick to turn off the political debate on the tube and smiled back at his little girl. "Feeling good?"

"Oh yes!" She'd decided to act on the side of subtlety, as if she was *just* containing herself.

It was the perfect response. Flexing her feet, stretching her legs somewhat, these helped the performance as well.

"Oh, good," her mom said. She was 38 years *old*, and although she'd kept her figure, it wasn't anywhere close by. "He used a condom?" she whispered.

Did he? Was he suppo –

Janie nodded, into the narrow path of least resistance. Dad wanted to follow up with a statement or some small talk, but he didn't have any that wouldn't embarrass himself.

The three left, seeing no one but a maid in the hall. She was wearing an outdated black and white uniform, and smiled and waved at them, as if she was just passing but believed that someone should say goodbye.

Lyi watched from the stairs. The grin on his face was hidden in the hall shadows. He went back to his room for the night, determined to see the end of Laure's performance. The hard dick in his pants had already throbbed out all traces of Janie. Yet something of her lingered. Perhaps it was the ass. Yes. It was similar to Laure's. Both smooth. *So* smooth looking.

He didn't need Janie to keep himself erect, not with all of Ms. Sainclair spread out on the couch, taking many inches of a Frenchman with perfect hair and glasses.

Why doesn't she ever take the facial? he thought to himself. *All that in the ass yet afraid to...*

It didn't matter to the story of *First Lady*. Lyi kept his cock up for many minutes, always saving himself from a conclusion. Always not quite watching to the end, but slowing down before the pop shot. He could make himself last a good 40 minutes with French. 80 to 120 with Asian. Russian could be chancy...

"Lyi!" Maugham bellowed from nearby.

He came. Just to cum. And had finished cumming by the time Maugham was at the thin piece of wood they called doors there. He unlocked it and let her gargantuan boss self in. He thought of Natalie Wood as he spoke to her. Just to think of Natalie Wood.

"What are you *doing*?" she screamed.

He just realized; he *hadn't* finished yet. "Shhiiiiiiitt!!" He got some gunk on her. He stood, trying to retain Cool, shuffling his feet a little. It happened partly because of the threat – the promise – of being caught, this being the first time he'd cum with her watching. It was the excitement; he tried to explain that to her, which had only stimulated him more. It seems he was still hard. And could cum again, he knew, if he let himself. But there was something about her withering look... He just tried to cup the gushing cum in his hand, half to hide the throbbing, half to stop the flow, which went on and on, into his other hand. Not withering enough of a look, he thought. He didn't even have to pump cock to keep up.

In Maugham's hand was brand-name tissue. Or was it Bounty? Did he not notice her move to get it? He'd had his hands full. It was like a dream. Just not one he'd consciously choose.

"Can you stop that?" she moaned evenly.

He was still pulling on it. Lyi stopped immediately, wet hands to his sides. He went for the TV, to shut it, but since his hands were dripping, he merely succeeded in splashing a brunette's face on the screen with his liquid children.

Seething yet cool, Maugham took the remote from the bed, did the button, and threw it back among the pillows. "In my pouncey office, *now*!"

Lyi grabbed the Bounty with his teeth and she rolled off like a boulder. It wasn't enough paper. But it soaked the gist. He ran over to the other side of the bed, staining the gold box that contained more tissue with his fingers and wiped himself strategically. He could still feel the tingle, and wanted to jack again. The excitement. It would be *so* easy to get himself ready again, because he had to get himself downstairs, quickly, and didn't have *time* to jack, which only made him more and more horny. *The excitement...*

Maugham's yelling had knocked Sid and Armando from their hind quarters. Each stood in their jeweled doorways, like t-bones with their high shoulders, watching Lyi trundle down the pearl-railed stairs.

He came. Just to cum. And had finished cumming by the time Maugham was at the thin piece of wood they called doors there. He unlocked it and let her gargantuan boss self in. He thought of Natalie Wood as he spoke to her. Just to think of Natalie Wood.

depression, as she will. Unfucked, unloved. The Steels will look for cause and effect. They will take that female girl thing to the cunt doctor and he/she will go down on her and spy the damaged, being *intact*, hymen you fucking *left* there. And we'll have *all* our asses and placebos sued off. Can you get through college without your ass, Lyi?"

"You're overreacting."

"I don't agree you can," she said. "What would you sit on? There are so many seats in collegiate buildings, my man. In the theatre building alone – "

"They wouldn't *sue*."

"I would!" Maugham shouted. There were flecks of red in her eyes now. It was quite beautiful. "I would put Derek or Fripper on her hairy pee machine, but this is your lack of cock up, and you're going to mow the yard. Is that utterly?"

What?

"Fuck the bitch," she enunciated, her eyes straightening, "or you do not return."

It was July. It was hot. Traffic spilled into downtown Providence like a cackle of cranky cats, just released from their leashes. The bus jerked within the madness and contained just enough air conditioner to support life, though Lyi was still certain that the babe before him, clad in thong and seashell bra, would faint before they crossed 14th. Her nipples were sweating through and the half-dollar wideness of them reminded him faithfully of Janie's. God, she had wide nips too. Just not Ds. Janie's were B minus perhaps...

Since Lyi was at fault, Maugham wasn't springing for cabs. Though she did allow him the use of the house's handheld SatNav, which came in handy for locating the houses of girls so fucking ugly. Pricks with pizzas were using them all the time.

The Steel residence was like an apartment building except it was all theirs. Maugham had assured Lyi that knocking on *any* door would do. Which he did. A maid in disguise, just in regular clothes, answered.

"Can I see Janie?"

The middle-aged slave didn't ask to see any proof of anything, didn't ask any questions, just sidestepped so he could come on in.

They were in a thin lip of lobby or living room. The tower of rounding stairs, leading to many, many doors had inspired many a visitor. *Must've been a Ramada*, Lyi thought meekly.

All the maid or whoever she was did was point. A door on the second floor. Lyi climbed the curve of stairs, staring at his feet to make sure he didn't tumble, but didn't see Janie at the foot of them. She pulled at his arm, keeping the pressure hard until she pushed him into her mammoth room. It was all pink and in the corner was a Christmas tree tickled with Transformers figures. Toward the far wall was a shiitake mushroom-shaped, squat bed with balloon and troll-shaped pillows chronically infesting it.

"Did Maugham tell you I was coming?" he asked once the shock died down. She'd asked him a couple urgent questions before that, but they couldn't penetrate the distraction of her inner chamber.

"No one *told* me."

"That woman downstairs just let me in!"

"Just now?"

"I mean," Lyi struggled, "she didn't ask for ID or anything!"

"So?"

After several moments, Lyi nodded. Even understood. He led her to the edge of the bed and relocated some trolls so they could sit, backs against the wall. "If I don't get you fucked," he explained slowly, astutely, "I could lose my job." He left that to simmer a moment. The continued the good news: "You don't have to get it. Just back me up. Say… I liked you, which I do. I came over. We went out. Where are your parents?"

"That's dangerous, Janie!"

She gave him that *stupid fool* look girls save for boys, and behind it was a pang of appreciation. "What are you *doing* here?"

"They *know* you didn't get fucked?"

"What? What do you mean 'they know'?"

"Like, *knowledge*. They *know*."

There was panic between her teeth. "How do they 'know'?"

"However they know. So, I need to stay here a while. And you come with me and swear we did it and all's w – "

"I can't *go with* you!"

"It's been done. In your parents' eyes. What does it matter, going back?"

This required Duffy clutching. Her favorite, current teddy bear – Duffy, the Disney bear, from her trip to Tokyo DisneySea six years ago. She was a mere twelve years old and the exotic mix of black pepper popcorn, seeing the ocean from the second floor of Cinderella Castle and getting a China-made bear that everyone else had had been so surreal. Amazing. Superspecial. One of the few times she had such a good time with her parents, since they spent most of their time apart. *This* was the bear to hug now. Duffy had little stuffing left, not in these teenage years.

"They would know I lied," she said quietly.

After several moments, Lyi nodded. Even understood. He led her to the edge of the bed and relocated some trolls so they could sit, backs against the wall. "If I don't get you fucked," he explained slowly, astutely, "I could lose my job." He left that to simmer a moment. The continued the good news: "You don't have to get it. Just back me up. Say… I liked you, which I do. I came over. We went out. Where are your parents?"

"In the car."

"In the car!"

Janie was starting to cry. Starting to try not to cry.

Lyi had to ask, "What are they doing in the car?"

Janie shrugged and Lyi chalked it up to the behavior of rich people. He didn't want to push her to tears. This wasn't going well.

"Come on." He was pulling at her. "Let's go get pizza."

"I can't leave the *house*!"

In the end, they sat on the terrace overlooking night traffic. The highway stirred up a fantastic breeze that wouldn't leave them alone. The thin Russian cook downstairs did them a Virginia ham, summer cabbage and yellow pepper pizza with no cheese and the sweetest basil tomato sauce Lyi had ever had. A servant knocked and left it just outside the door.

The boy ate and looked at the girl when she wasn't doing the same.

"You like your job?"

"Oh yeah," he said. "All that fresh young pussy. It's great."

"Aren't they all ugly? Isn't that the prerequisite?"

"Every girl is pretty inside. The pink is pretty. You like pink, don't you?"

"Pink is cool. If you're a girl!"

"Aren't you a girl?"

"I'm a young lady."

He looked at her. "Let's get out of here. Grab a real pizza. This one's too good."

It was, she had to admit. It was perfection, no grease or preservatives. It was junk.

They hopped out the window and snuck down Pounce Circle, their shoes making little dirt clouds. Just a few turns down a slight road they found My's Pizza. It was layered with cig smoke and littered with the kinds of eaters who might go for flesh, if the pizzas took too long.

Barely looking, Lyi pointed at his choice at the very top, the most expensive pizza on the menu, the one with the longest description, which he didn't read. "And a picture of Pepsi."

The buffalo-faced waitress showed him the picture of a pitcher of Pepsi on the back of the menu. "That's it," Lyi said, explaining they'd split it, and she left to do their bidding.

Janie was having trouble with the smoke, mostly around her eyes. But the more they talked, the more she forgot everything, even the smoke. She remembered how to smile.

"You go to school?"

She nodded. "It sucks. It's all about population and popularity."

"How is it about population?"

"It isn't really." She shrugged. All the men were staring at them, she was so ugly.

"It sounded good."

"Thanks."

"You probably meant subliminally stacking up friends," the boy said. "The more friends, the greater your throng, the more popular."

"Yeah, that's it."

"I'm going to be a dentist. Though it's really hard for me to concentrate these days. The money's shit. The pussy is so sweet."

"You know I'm sitting right here, right?"

"What do you mean?" he asked.

"Sweet pussy."

He could tell she was upset, just not sure why. "I'm sorry. You want to talk about something else?"

"Yeah!"

"It's just business."

"Then I don't like business!"

When the pizza appeared, they ate in silence and smoke. The thing was covered in so much pepperoni, they had to lift pieces to find other toppings, which they mostly picked at and ate. It was thin and crispy. Janie went for snatches of the crust – a banana pepper – snatches of crust – a piece of corn. Everyone watched them. Lyi took Janie's greasy hand and helped her put it to her mouth. She didn't need any help. Her eyes bulged at him while she removed a snatch of crust without looking at it. He smiled at her, but she'd run out of smile.

"Are you okay?"
"I'm charming," he said.
"Yeah?"
"You like me."
She did. It was fact. "I like you."
"Why?"
She thought about it. "You're nice."
"Did you like my cock?"
"What's that?"
That threw him for a loop. "My cock. My dick."

"Oh! Sorry. It came out of nowhere. Why are you asking me that?"

"I – I don't know." He waited. "Did you know that guys think about sex every six seconds?"

The pitcher came late. Two huge straws and no glass. Lyi was parched.

"You mean *every* guy?" she asked, eyes red and round.

"Well. Yeah. Not collectively."

"Why?"

"We have testosterone. It grows us hair here." He rubbed his smooth face. "It's also what keeps us from living as long as you."

"That's not good."

Lyi shrugged. "I think it's a fair trade. Pussy is *so* sweet."

"Are you going to keep talking about pussy?"

"I'm sorry." The check came and the boy used a cum-stained twenty to get them out of there. They walked, filling their lungs with slightly fresher Rhode Island air. Her arm was in his. It was warm for July. They stepped in the middle of a crap bridge and watched boring ducks. "Why don't you like pussy?"

"God!"

"I'm just making conversation."

"You're sex mad! It can't be that important!"

"It fucking *is*."

"You don't have to curse," she said, but didn't take her arm away.

"Oh..."

"What?"

"You're one of *those* girls."

"I'm not."

"What girls?" he asked.

"What you said."

"All I said was those girls," he hardly explained. "What am I saying?"

"*I'm* saying can't we talk about *normal* things? Pussy isn't normal. And I don't care if every girl has one."

"I'm sorry." The check came and the boy used a cum-stained twenty to get them out of there. They walked, filling their lungs with slightly fresher Rhode Island air. Her arm was in his. It was warm for July. They stepped in the middle of a crap bridge and watched boring ducks. "Why don't you like pussy?"

They were making their slow way towards the machine that gave a handful of duck food for a quarter. They were by the stream everyone called the river. Janie sprung for it. It looked like dog food.

"Is this your first, like, date?" Lyi asked her.

She gave him two pieces of dog food, picked up with long, straight fingers but made no comment.

Down the hilly, cobbly road was an antique "palace" where everyone brought their tat on consignment. Lyi made for there while he tried to hold Janie's fidgety hand. He kept looking at her young Raquel Welch form that she hid so well. Her clothes clung to things. Not *really*. But he knew what was beneath them. He could see with his mind.

"Why did your parents want you fucked so bad?"

She said nothing, so Lyi internalized for non-work related subjects. He wished she spoke more.

Maybe she didn't *need* noise. Like he did. So he just waited.

They browsed the old stuff in the palace, which was like a maze put up by grandmothers. Sometimes Janie would point at a poster and relate to the ancient Coke baby in terms of Coldplay or Thor or Michelle Obama. Lyi had nothing to say about the plates she found cute or the old one-eyed cat the size of a gumball machine that sat like a sandbag by the register. All he could think about was ass and pussy and how he'd loved to play connect the dots with the zits of her facial.

"Will you buy this for me?" she asked, holding up a primordial coffee bean grinder.

"Aren't your parents rich?"

He didn't get it, so she put it down and moved on. Lyi took it up again, just to look, but kept it in his arms. He didn't bother keeping it hidden. She smiled back at him when she saw.

There were some farmhouse puzzles in old boxes that may have had all the pieces. When Janie hovered over them a few minutes, Lyi picked one up at random. It showed stupid people having a picnic too close to a lot of happy geese.

There were some farmhouse puzzles in old boxes that may have had all the pieces. When Janie hovered over them a few minutes, Lyi picked one up at random. It showed stupid people having a picnic too close to a lot of happy geese.

By the time they were ready to check out, his arms were full and light feeling when he put all the junk on the counter. $86.10. He paid it gladly. Janie's smile was wide.

Her eyes went to the ground much of the way home. The boy thought of her pussy, as boys do, and how hairy it was... In his heart of hearts he knew she'd never shaved in her life and would be one of those "but it itches" girls.

"Thanks," she suddenly said, stopping.

It was dark. They were by the fence to her property, between the business mailbox and the sidewalk filled with gloomy tree shadows.

"Can I come inside?" Though he meant it just the one way, he couldn't help thinking of both ways.

"Dad is going to blast."

"I met him. He seems nice."

"He's going to hate *you.*"

"Why? He brought you to me."

In her most terrible Dad accent, she spewed, "*That's the man who fucked my daughter!*"

Lyi impersonated himself: "And I fell in love with her immediately."

Still Dad: "*You can't fall in love with her like that, boy!*"

"Oh, but I can. Her pussy was so sweet. It was like licking watermelon stamps."

She laughed. "*What are you trying to say, boy!*"

"I want to fuck her again, and again, Mr. Steel. May I?"

"*I'll have no more talk of p here, you dolt!*"

"If you could know for yourself – "

"*Back! Back to your house of…*"

She didn't know what to call a house of ill repute, so the joke broke and the two of them laughed like it was the funniest thing on the block, which it was.

After Lyi wiped his eyes, he asked quickly, "When can I see you again?"

There was shock. It was so out of the blue.

Then the shock left, and all she had was thought. She thought. "I don't like the piano," she muttered.

Out of the blue to him, too. "Really? That's – "

"I have to take lessons on Tuesdays and Fridays. Then, let's make a mall of it. Meet you at the Appleby's entrance at 4?"

"Great! This Friday then."

"Sure."

Unknown to her, Janie did a little two-step dance that Lyi knew well. Her panties were wet. Had to be. She adjusted herself by stepping needlessly. He couldn't see the cameltoe, but…

"We could even have dinner there," he said.

"At the *mall*?" There was something amazing in the way she said it.

"Do you think we could fuck?"

"God!"

"Not *during* dinner."

Janie filed her arms with the stuff he carried for her and bounded toward the building. She didn't rush. She wasn't nervous. But she ignored him beautifully.

Lyi checked into the nearest La Quinta, knowing he couldn't check back in to Maugham's place, no, not that same night. He bought teeth cleaning stuff at Rite Aid, some cheap Puritan clothes at Walmart, and stayed in, wanking to thoughts of Janie's tight young form. In his mind, she did splits and smiled and cooed and sucked anyone's cock and did slow jumping jacks, sometimes on a pool cue, sometimes not.

His hand was still on himself, all naked, the next morning when the maid knocked as she entered.

She showed no surprised, and seemed to care even less. She wasn't gifted in the face, so Lyi took a biz card from his wallet that had fallen out of his pants, and said, "Remember me to your daughter."

He got dressed as she hoovered and scampered over to Janie's, hoping to catch her on her way to high school or whatever rich girls did.

He waited, but she didn't show, not in any car that turned a corner. He must have missed her. The breeze was cool from the south. There was a promise of honeydew ice cream within view, so Lyi sauntered over to the ice cream van, trying to keep Maugham and scolding thoughts out of his head.

She giggled at him when he sauntered to the counter side of the van.

"I've been watching you!" Janie said, empty Co-Cone wrapper in hand. Not much had the power to turn Ly's head red, but this did it.

He sat on the curb and the van moved away. There was that vague feeling of loss from not ordering ice cream. But more importantly, there was Janie. And without a bra. A 34, he was *sure*.

"You haven't been here *all* this time?"

"Why not?" she answered.

"You couldn't see me. The ice cream – "

"I was hiding behind the parked cars."

"Why?"

They stared at the massive dwelling that was Janie's home.

"You must like me," he finally said. The wind whipped his brown hair until it went back to just how it always was.

"I've noticed you."

"You skipped school for me."

"Don't be a toe! I always skip school."

"Really?"

"No," Janie admitted. "This is my first time."

He eyed her. The wind was unwrapping her hair. And her nips were slowly rising. "Why is that?"

Without an answer, Lyi merely applied pressure to her arm and they went around the steep corner, south into the wind towards civilization. There was a candy store called Glom's. On its sun-glistening windows were posters promising chocolate-covered plastic dishes of ice cream. They sat at one of twelve empty tables and ordered and ate ice cream, talking about the good old days of yesterday and now. How cold it was. How the lady dipped Lyi's cone in the strawberry and what caused hardness. Janie noticed that the only hardness he mentioned was the strawberry coating.

They postulated why drinking melted ice cream was muddy and wrong. Talked of how hot the day was, how cool the clouds looked. They walked to the unused metal bleachers where weekend teams pretended baseball and football were interesting. Lyi removed his shirt to show off his muscles and paunch and to give his woman protection from the morning due that hadn't yet evaporated. They sat.

The boy flexed silently and said, "What should be done with your first breath of freedom?"

"We could see *Salt*. You like Jolie?"

He shrugged. "I don't do much mainstream. You like Draghixa?"

"Who's that?"

"She – " He stopped. Birds visited the tree closest. Girls must like birds. She was watching the little red-trunk robin and so he pretended to be interested in its song, though he really was.

It reminded her. "Do you have any hobbies?"

"I like – "

She held up a hand, but smiled. "Can we have a normal conversation?"

"What's normal?"

"Like…" She aimed her hand at the birds.

"Who talks about birds?"

"Who talks about p all the time?"

"You can't even say it."

"So?"

"It's part of *you*. It's just a word."

"It's a dirty word," Janie said. So said her mom. Once. Getting out of the shower. But it made an impact.

Janie didn't want the morning spoiled. She didn't want to leave this place.

"A word can't be dirty. You can say anything. You can say anything you want to say. There is no cunt police. If *you* don't think it's wrong, it's not wrong. Unless you hurt someone with your words."

"*You're* hurting *me*."

There was the sound of the bird.

Though no one moved, the boy said, "You're not leaving."

"No fucking pussy, okay?"

Lyi was impressed. He could almost see a full layer of shell fall off her. Yet, in the back of his mind, he wondered if *fucking* was a verb or an adjective. "Wow."

"Wow," she agreed. But it had already left her mind. It wasn't a victory.

They watched trees. They watched trees unwinding in the wind. They tried watching the wind.

"Why don't you want to fuck me?" he asked all of a sudden.

"Could you stop saying f?"

"Fuck you!" And he held her quickly, in case she didn't embrace the joke, the very serious joke, in case she ran away. She crawled into the hug quite quickly then. No thoughts. Just let herself melt in that tepid morning.

The embrace was like fumbling in rope, and soon merged into plain closeness. Body on body.

"I don't know why you want me anyway," she said, clutched and clutching. "I look like tear gas."

"Tear gas! How does that look?"

The girl scrunched up her face like a burn victim. Then released it back to normal. The screwed up eyes, the bicycle basket of a mouth, her uneven eyebrows all meant nothing to Lyi.

"It's a dirty word," Janie said. So said her mom. Once. Getting out of the shower. But it made an impact.

Janie didn't want the morning spoiled. She didn't want to leave this place.

"A word can't be dirty. You can say anything. You can say anything you want to say. There is no cunt police. If you don't think it's wrong, it's not wrong. Unless you hurt someone with your words."

"You're hurting me."

There was the sound of the bird.

"I like you."

"Why?"

"Why?"

"I'm not likeable."

"You're hot."

"I'm not!" She didn't want him to let go. All their muscles were tense.

"You are! You have a *fantastic* body. Remember, this is the guy who's seen it! And I've seen more than one body."

"You just want me to say you fucked me."

After a second, Lyi unclutched and stood. "Wow." He walked a little.

"I'm sorry!"

She ran after him. He was just standing there. She gridlocked her hand in his.

He patted it. "I know. You're 18. You're still in high school."

"Still? I'm graduating!"

"I mean… you need more confidence in you."

She hung her head and let herself be led.

"Especially," Lyi continued, "in your natural talents. You've got the fuck body – no, let me say fuck, please." She'd squeezed his hand. He massaged her palm with constant movement and love. "You've got naturals. I'm a direct guy. You're gonna find that truth is a *good* thing. And I don't mean anything *by* it.

"You've got this… killer, 18-year-old body. And you're hiding it like a bra. Bras are so useless. You're hiding your *perfect* tits – succulent cunt – like… a wig. When you've *got* the hair. You know?"

She shook her head with force, so he took it in both hands and slowed it down.

"I'm serious!"

She looked at him. *He probably believes it.*

"I wanted to save myself for…"

"I know."

They walked. It was the afternoon. There were flecks of water in the air, air on the verge of becoming so clean. When they parted, there was only the smell of moisture. The rumbling of the clouds followed Lyi back to the only place he didn't want to go. But it held all his stuff, rubbers, and tomorrow was pay day.

Luck was with him; Maugham was at the bank. Lyi lit up for a shower, fresh clothes, he brushed his various hairs with the pink brush Britney Spears' ugly personal assistant had given him. She'd swallowed, so he kept the brush.

Rand poked his head in while Lyi still had his shirt off. "Mom's running around with her panties down."

"I'd like to see that."

"You've got this… killer, 18-year-old body. And you're hiding it like a bra. Bras are so useless. You're hiding your perfect tits – succulent cunt – like… a wig. When you've got the hair. You know?"

"What did you do, man?"

He pushed past Rand, who touched his shoulder, and knocked on Dav's door. He waited for "come" and did.

Dav was the only 40+ in the facilities. Body and face of a 25-year-old, he didn't have lines in his face, still had abs and all his hair, and was usually on hand for parents and fuckees who preferred the sage, mature form.

"Can you grab my check for me, man?"

Dav was slowly masturbating in the dark, per usual. He didn't have television, didn't believe in it. Just a wall of conquest photos and a fine memory. Lyi liked him best. He wasn't screwy or creepy or full of "the movement" or of himself, opinions, crap, he just liked to cum, near or inside young ladies, and had found his calling.

"No prob," Dav said, waving the other hand. "You're in the shit."

"No."

"You didn't fuck that pussy?"

"I'm working on it," and Lyi started to close the door.

"Things happen when you don't force 'em," he said , and laughed as the door closed.

Yeah, Lyi thought, it *is* funny.

Maugham – the boys called her Mom because she was no MILF – was waiting. Her office door was open and she was glaring at the boy. A reprieve: there was a family of butt uglies in her office just then, so Maugham wasn't about to chew him out now. She just handed Lyi a piece of paper and shut the door in his face. A wave of A/C hit him and it felt good.

It wasn't a company check, just a tri-folded, typed letter. (Some of the boys did odd jobs around the house when they weren't fucking ugly girls. Since Maugham paid by the hour not by the pussy. Lyi thought this might be a list of duties, now that his dick was off duty. Howard could type 70 wpm, so he was unofficial secretary. According to him, when he wasn't fucking anything, Mom never asked him for a clit lick. Ever. However *she* got off, it wasn't from odd job men. Either she was a dyke or she was past that age and this was just a business to her. Thus, was the letter typed.)

> *Dear Fucking Whore –*
>
> *Would it surprise your cracked ass to discern that the Steels have indeed started shaving the very life from under me? Law, suits. Lawsuit! No change. Which means, tender wank, no cash for baby. If I get popped, you get a can of enormous worms in your bed.*
>
> *Tell me why I'm not firing you, or 40% off your next dick dips until my bank and psyche have been smoothed. Right?*
>
> *Love,*
>
> *Hate*

Lyi deciphered it fine, and decided to see Janie's parents.

Walking, thinking, he'd easily agree to take 60% just to keep his job. For as long as it took to pay off his part of the mess. If it went that far. Just… the whole situation was unfair. It was between him and her, why, how did anyone else *know*? Was Janie lying to him? He only just came on the scene. Some of these rich daughter/mom combos could be tight, he heard. Maybe she tells Mom everything. Maybe Mom is a slag. He'd try the Dad first.

Janie was waiting for him on the steps. Waiting for *him*, because when she saw him, she jumped up and ran to and unlocked the gate.

Swinging it open, she blurted, "You can't come in!"

"They're suing the house!"

"I know."

She was wearing a tight, stripped cardigan that hugged what she had and borrowed.

For a change Lyi was not swayed by tightness, and brushed past her forcibly, up the steps to the locked door. He turned back to her.

"Can you open this?"

"You're under no litigation, it's just the company."

"I don't care. Did you tell them why?"

"Why?"

"Why I didn't fuck the *shit* out of you. I would have."

"I mean, *why* would I tell them that?"

"It's the truth?" Her form looked so good. So soft, so gentle – it could be crushed like an orphan marshmallow so easily. Lyi tried to let a kind spirit rise, but it stayed in his shoes and sulked. "Saving yourself. That's a noble thing, isn't it?"

"Daddy just wants me fucked," she said simply. Her voice was so small.

"I want to see him."

He tried the door, forgetting he had already. It rattled. Lyi came close to Janie, put his big Irish hands in her jeans pockets.

Being that close. Not looking her in the face. Squooshing that terribly pregnant shirt that bunched up in front as she leaned over as if he was hurting her. She rose and the tightness returned to find the curves in her body. He said to her perfect 34s, "I'd sure like to fuck you hard."

Janie sighed. She gave up. "I guess that's the difference between us."

"You want to *make love*."

Her eyes went wide. "How'd you know that?"

Lyi's mouth was a thin pink line. "When you stop hearing the *words* and hear what I'm saying, you'll know the difference."

She wanted to say something, it didn't even have to be wise and wonderful, but she just didn't have the practice for emotional parrying. It drained her. Even seeing the house keys in his hand, him going into the darkened hallway, door closing, she did nothing.

She sat on the step.

Mr. Steel worked from home in a suit and tie doing high-priced things on computers, printers, copiers. The whole office, bigger than a library, was air conditioned within an inch of its life. There was a rack for coats by the door with a sign at the top saying Take One.

Lyi took a coat and edged his socks up further before stepping into the cold, dull room bathed in the red of filtered sun through shades.

"What do *you* want?" came a voice.

"It's about your daughter," Lyi told the echo.

"She's my wife's daughter today. Very bad girl."

"I know. I mean, I don't think so. I'm the guy who fucked her."

There was a moment's typing, then the sound of good shoes on a lacquered floor. The Father, thin and unlovely, came forth from the metal bookcases in the middle of the shadowy floor. Maybe 20% of his homeliness sprouted from the disdain he wore. Still,

Lyi could see here was the poor ugly tree Janie was clinging to. Crinkled brow, wicked open mouth, he was simply hard to look at without the make-up he used for outside excursions.

"You didn't fuck *my* daughter," he said with confidence.

Lyi shook his head forward as a bluffing man in the right will. "I beg to differ, sir. I was there."

The Father stood a moment. He was neither one way nor the other. "You're a liar."

"Wow!"

He counted his fingers. "In the first place, she has this hymen hang-up, I don't believe you could do it. Without the fantasy of 'first time' I do believe she could amount to something. Get on with her beautiful young life. She's so *attractive* on the inside."

He counted his fingers. "In the first place, she has this hymen hang-up, I don't believe you could do it. Without the fantasy of 'first time' I do believe she could amount to something. Get on with her beautiful young life. She's so attractive on the inside."

"Yeah. But I fucked her."

"Why would you tell me that?"

"Fucked the shit out of her!"

"Got it on tape, goombah. What do you think?"

All the color drained from Lyi's face. "*Tape?*"

"MP4, then. Well, it's an avi file. I didn't get myself off on it, but it's in my hard drive. Want to see? Do you *want* to see how you *didn't* fuck Janie?"

Lyi's redness refused to subside. He was hot. But he decided to move with the times. "She's saving herself, you know."

"I don't *care* what she wants," the Father said, sitting on some books. "That's what I pay you people for."

"Why do you want her fucked so badly?"

"I don't care how you *do* it."

"I mean," Lyi explained slower, "why do you so badly want her fucked? She's a – "

"She's ugly as fuck! How else is it going to happen? And it's none of your business. You should've moralized before you got undressed. It would've been a different man, maybe an older man, and we wouldn't have the hymen we have now!"

"She doesn't need – "

"No." There was a time in every deal when Mr. Steel closed up rational shop and went home. That time was now. "Go home. Save your money. I'll close Maugham's place for this. You can't renege a deal. You can't drive hopes up. We'll have to go up to Maine to get her fucked now. It's all inconvenient…"

"I – Janie and I – "

"No! I know a boy. Fuck the professionals. Friend of mine. Don't worry about it anymore. Just get out."

"Janie and I – "

"No!"

The Father was wearing a glove remote, he always did, and clicked it softly to call for the gorilla in the kitchen who was chopping vegetables. In came the mountain of man to escort young Lyi out without threats.

The gate went click and Lyi saw red. All the way home. He stormed into Maugham's office without warning. She was signing checks, listening to "Rudy Red Dress" by Helen Reddy.

"You're *taping* us?" yelled Lyi.

"How did you get in?"

"*Taping* us? *Why*?"

"The door was locked!" She knew it wasn't, but she believed in shouting fire with fire.

"No, it wasn't! Have you always done this? Huh?"

Maugham was checking the doorknob, assembling her thoughts. "If you broke this…"

"Break your fucking ass!"

"It's in your freelance contract, dumb mouth!" She wasn't going to show him the contract *now*, not even if he asked to see it again. No telling what else he'd find if he chose to study it.

"My contract?"

"Not that it matters. With the biz-i-ness falling to shit. In the toilet. Flushed. Like a Civil War whore on a hot day."

Lyi was livid, and wasn't going for it. "I'm not feeling sorry for you!"

"Then feel sorry for yourself!"

He'd had enough. *Finally enough*. Lyi picked his way through the straights and the gays assembled in the hall, all secretly loving the noise. He had his bag packed in seven minutes. Mostly colored underwear and Marc Dorcel DVDs. Most of what he didn't need lay still and scattered around the warm room. He had enough saved. He just wanted out.

No one said goodbye, "don't go." No one, not even Maugham, was there to block his path. "You're too valuable!" No, there was none of that, knowing there were ten cocks ready for every vacancy, and it was depressing waiting for the bus with those oppressive memories lingering.

It would've been nice if Janie had walked right by there. Janie, especially the tight bottom half, Janie below the neck, Janie, who's lovely cunny had never been trimmed and obviously never needed to be.

It would've been nice if Janie had walked right by there. Janie, especially the tight bottom half, Janie below the neck, Janie, who's lovely cunny had never been trimmed and obviously never needed to be.

Lyi found himself on the bus to nowhere within 10 minutes. He just got on the next one. The lady at the counter told him where he was going and he'd paid attention then, but unpopularity engulfed him and now, comfortable, air conditioned in the Rhode Island summer, Lyi wondered where he'd end up.

"I won't go!"

"You will!"

James Lestivi, brown from hair to toe, abs like a puzzle, arms like poplar trees, sat on the bed, playing with himself because he couldn't find the remote and girls usually liked it if you're standing twice when they entered the room.

Moments later there was screaming, ranting, louder and higher. Clawing in the hall, foul words, a slap, heavy trodding on the rug just outside. A girl, half naked, all panting, half her tits on view, was thrown in the room like something caught. The door locked quickly and little Janie pounded on it. She choked the knob to try to get it to open. She cursed, she kicked it.

Then she turned to James. Seething. Never in her life had she been as *confident* as in this moment. "You are *not* fucking this!"

He looked to where she pointed. Half her shirt was gone. He could see some twat.

"Hi. My name's James. Would you like a drink?"

"You are *not* fucking this." She tore away at the rest of her dress. Tore her panties off. And braced herself.

"You don't need to be nervous."

"*Fuck you!*"

"Hey!" He frowned. It was *supposed* to be difficult, he told himself. Gay guys are so much easier. "I think you'd relax if you had a drink."

"I'd relax more if you had a fucking neck."

"You don't need to insult me."

"Somebody needs to!"

"Don't be a bitch. Come on." He padded the bed.

"You play football, don't you?"

"Yeah. I was – "

"I fucking thought so. All the intelligence is in your *fucking neck*, which is why you don't have one."

This wasn't fun anymore. James pressed a hidden button in the wall and waited. He tried smiling but he didn't have the vocabulary for it.

"Well?!" Janie shouted.

There was a knock at the door, and the girl readied herself to pounce on whoever opened it.

It was the door of a dumb waiter that opened. A trio of fizzy ice drinks were on a pewter tray. James put on his happy face, put the three drinks in the room and picked up two. One glass had a gold handle. This he left untouched. "You don't have to drink it. It's a little date rape drug in an Archie. That's got pineapple, soda, a stick of Juicy Fruit at the bottom – "

"I don't want to be fucked!"

"What?"

"Where's Lyi? I want Lyi to fuck me!"

"But it's free." He looked at her like a football player. Gravity was dragging his dick down. "Why am I here?"

"Because you're a fucking *asshole!!!*" And being unused to foul mouthing, Janie just repeated herself over and over. James fumed himself into a lax penis and left. Janie had the run of the place, finally.

"Where's Lyi?" she asked every dick in the place, running into the hall. Most doors were open. It was Tuesday, the off day. Most of the dicks stood in their doorways shaking only their heads.

Dav came out of the bathroom, a '79 Penthouse in hand. "Janie!"

The girl spun around accusingly. She was still naked. "Where's Lyi?"

"Did you get fucked?"

"Shut up!"

He laughed, but not with teeth. "Yeah, I recognized you right away, you ugly girl. Ha ha, I'm kidding. He talks about nothing else these days – "

"Where *is* he?"

"Huh. I thought he'd be out back pumping that." He pointed to her pussy. Which did look fresh, perfectly formed and inviting. Janie knew she should be embarrassed, but reality was too whacked right now.

"Where *is* he?"

"I don't know!" He clutched her elbow, but she broke away like a dog without a license. "No, come in my room a minute."

"So you can *fuck* me?"

It wasn't a bad idea. He had the expert eye of changing jeans to nudity without using much imagination, and she was *skin*, but, "No, I got – " He wanted to whisper the reason but she wasn't letting anyone close enough. They all wanted the same fucking thing.

"In my pad," he said forcibly. Using his age, to command a little respect. "Please. It's about Lyi."

"Nothing's going in my body."

"My word."

She followed him in and skipped to the back of the room while he locked the door. That was worrying. But he only stood there, at the door. "I don't know where the fuck he's gone."

"Yeah?"

"Have you ever sucked cock, Janie?"

"Okay."

"It's really tasty. Some women tell me – "

"I want to leave."

" – it tastes just like pineapple." He waited. "I'm serious with you!"

"You want to let me pass?"

"What I want. Is your head in a bag, for stealing my mate, and that." He pointed at her muffin. "Around the thick girth of my dick. It's a fair trade."

She was only angry now. "For fucking *what*?"

"I think I know where he's going," Dav said quietly.

"Where? Who? Lyi? Where?"

Dav spread his hands out. "You need to get fucked. To be a real woman." When she sighed in pain, he continued, "You don't understand! You don't understand your own body. You can't know love until you *make* it."

"I'm here," she said patiently, "so Maugham won't get closed down."

"What? What?" Dav lost what little flippancy and gamesmanship he was expending in an instant. Suddenly things seemed more serious.

Maybe... Janie thought a moment. "You can save all of them and you can be a hero. You can get me out of here. You never have to worry about anything again."

"What?"

"Come down to the office," she said, maneuvering toward the door. "Tell the boss you fucked me. It's over. I'm gone..."

It wasn't a bad idea. He had the expert eye of changing jeans to nudity without using much imagination, and she was skin, but, "No, I got – " He wanted to whisper the reason but she wasn't letting anyone close enough. They all wanted the same fucking thing.

The sheepishness on Dav's face let all the gas out of her balloon. He started to touch her, then asked, "Can I touch you?"

"Where?"

"On the elbow."

"Okay."

He led her by the elbow into the bathroom where he immediately turned on the faucet, and aged and changed. "I really wish you hadn't said that."

"Said what?"

"This whole place is wired in stereo and Blu-ray. Maugham's an Asian licenser for a group of upwards of 50 websites."

"Wha – ? What are you talking about?"

"There's a fetish for fucking ugly and fat girls. Okay?"

Fetish and Blu-ray went together in her mind, and truth dawned, slow like the sun. "You mean – porn?"

"Right, porn. The only – "

"I don't want to be a porn star!"

"Haha, I wouldn't worry there, child. The only – "

Janie screamed, and started to cry.

"No, no!"

But she cried anyway. Dav rushed ahead: "Maugham isn't a *bad* mad babe. She does cut you in if you find out about it. Lyi didn't know. Not until yesterday. With you. That's why he quit!"

Dav kept flushing the toilet, so it was a little hard to hear. The girl's sniffles began to recede, and her tears were already drying. Blue water was filling up the toilet bowl. "Because of *me*?"

Dav nodded. "He quit because of fucking you. I mean, because of you."

"Where did he go?"

"He could've went to see Joe, his brother, in Portsmouth, but I don't know."

"Really?"

"I really don't. He could've. I'm not saying he did."

"Could I have his address?"

He gave it to her. Now, here in the bathroom, she liked this guy.

"Listen," she said while thinking it, "I'll give you a thousand dollars if you say you did me."

"Did you?"

"I will."

"No, I mean – "

"F me," she explained.

Dav smiled. Then laughed. "You had no problem with saying fucking before."

"I was tense. I was on edge. Come on."

Dav was shaking his head. "It's too late. Maugham's sure to be watching your every move. Down the halls. In my room. After what you said…"

"She's… also being sued, right? By my parents?"

The implication was clear. Dav gave the girl some baggy (on her) jeans and a yellow shirt that said Scream If You Love To Scream and they went down the stairs to blackmail someone.

"I fucked her," Dav said.

Maugham looked at the two of them. She was swirling a glass of fish-shaped ice cubes rolling in the thinnest bit of brown liquid. "I couldn't see that from here."

"I'll sue you myself if you don't do this," Janie said. "My ass in Asia!"

"You might do that," said Maugham, "but your parents want proof now."

"Her dad's not going to sit down with popcorn and watch that cherry get popped," Dav said. "Next girl who comes in with Janie's general hotness and color, we give them the edited .mov file of some competent fucking. You know."

Maugham was thinking. "Dark room. Dav calls your name. Your parents watch it, so what? You walk around a few days like you've been fucked." She started nodding.

"So?"

"I want a thousand bucks too."

"You want closed down!" Janie yelled. "I could fuck every guy in the *place* and you could still get your ass closed down if you aren't nice to *me*!"

Maugham thought about it. She stood, and spoke to Dav. "What's Dr. Caterwall going to say *this* time when he reaches in for that hymen and – "

"A thousand for him too." She held Maugham in a steady gaze. "Anything else?"

For the first time in her sordid life Maugham *had* nothing more to say. She retrieved the Steel contract from the files on her desk and looked at the blank lines of Fucked and Fucker. There were two copies already. Already copied long ago when the fuck had seemed so simple.

She turned the contracts around to show Janie, then motioned to a pen; a black dick-shaped pen in a white twat holder. It was only a simple paragraph, and in no legal jargon. Janie read through it quickly, checking to make sure that both pages were the same, and signed both. Maugham gave her the You've Been Fucked certificate, already pressed with a blue seal, embossed with gold lettering. With a kiss on Dav and a glare at Maugham, Janie was out of there.

She stopped by Portentia Tan and got herself a quickie five-minute, $25 "glow" and drove thru for some White Castles and went straight home.

"Her dad's not going to sit down with popcorn and watch that cherry get popped," Dav said. "Next girl who comes in with Janie's general hotness and color, we give them the edited .mov file of some competent fucking. You know."

Mr. Steel was so pleased, so excited. He already had the wood-screwed, oaken frame ready for the certificate, which he proudly paid a fortune for. He hugged his daughter and by the time he managed to get the wood screws set and the certification gleamed supinely on his office wall, little Janie was already at the airport to wait the four hours until the next flight out to *sort of near* Portsmouth. She listened to Bad English on her wireless mp3 player and tried to think thoughts.

She might give it up. She might keep it.

Nothing was planned.

GUIDELINES

WRITE FOR US! ART FOR US!

We are open to submissions year-round! If you are interested in writing for us or contributing artwork, please check out these guidelines or visit TheActItself.com:

The Act Itself is published three times a year in both print and ebook, sold both online and by subscription.

What We Are Looking For
In general, we're looking for fun, sexy stories and quality erotica artwork. We'll not consider anything which includes underage characters or stupidly dangerous acts. We will consider some fetish-oriented themes, but keep them light. This publication is to

bring everyone together, and for everyone to have a good time. What do we like to read in our spare time? Some of us enjoy *Penthouse Letters*, others like Literotica.com, others read the Marketplace books, or anything from Blue Moon. That should give you some idea as to what we're looking for. Fiction submissions should be sent as attachments to submissions@theactitself.com as either a MSWord or RTF file. Please make sure that you only send in a properly proofed version. Sloppy submissions are no good for anyone.

As for art, this will be – at least to start – a black & white publication, so images should have that taken into consideration. Go for sexy mood and suggestion. Go for beautiful form and enticing display. Avoid out and out hardcore porn. Sometimes what's not seen is more exciting than what's laid out on a slab. We'd like to see photography, drawings, and possibly even cartoons – although note that we're going to be tough on that last one especially. Blame *Playboy* for setting such a high bar for adult-themed cartoons. No manga or anime-styled artwork, please. Art submissions should be at least 300 dpi in TIF or JPG format. If you are having technical issues meeting this requirement, or have questions, feel free to contact the Managing Editor, John Teehan, at info@theactitself.com with questions. He's the helpful sort, he is.

Please do not simply direct us to your portfolio page, but e-mail us examples (or at the very least direct links to examples) of what you consider to be work best suited for this publication.

Got something else we've not mentioned but that you think might interest us? Feel free to query us at info@theactitself.com.

Details

- You must be over 21.
- You must furnish us with a 25 to 150-word bio.
- For fiction, send your name, email address, cover letter, story title, and completed manuscript to submissions@theactitself.com. (Please limit any art submissions to no more than three per e-mail and not to exceed a total of 5MB in size.) Please be patient, as we read Everything. We try to respond within 4 weeks.
- All additional queries and questions on advertising should be sent to our Managing Editor at info@theactitself.com.
- Your content must be original, must be yours, and not already in print or as an ebook. Yes, we check. We're actually fairly good at that.
- No simultaneous submissions please.
- Please keep submissions to less than 8,000 words. No novels, novellas or 2-parters.
- Upon acceptance, you will be required to sign a contract. Payment will be sent for your submission upon our receiving your signed contract. You will also be shown a PDF galley proof prior to publication. This will need to be reviewed promptly or it may miss its scheduled slot.

Payment and Rights

The Act Itself pays 3 cents per word for short stories up to 8,000 words stories, essays and interviews. $10 per photo/art accepted. Every contributor will also receive a free half-page ad (non-transferable) in the magazine for his book, art, CD or other item. (Please query first on sex toys.) We pay on acceptance. We require the work be original and that you have current control over any rights (i.e., if it is a work-for-hire piece purchased by another company, you may not have retained rights, please check).

For written material, we ask that you not publish your contribution elsewhere for a period of one year. After one year, complete rights are returned. In addition to our print and digital production, we reserve the right to republish your contribution as part of our audio issue collection, to be distributed by amazon, iTunes and others, for an additional $25 fee to you.

For artwork, rights are not subject to the exclusivity period.

Funds are paid in US currency. Contributors outside the US will be paid via PayPal. US contributors will be paid either via PayPal or check.

Reviews

Have a book, movie, game, or item you'd like to have considered for our review column? Contact info@theactitself.com for more information.

ADVERTISE WITH US

The Act Itself Introductory Ad Rate

Now is the time to take advantage of our special ad rates. Purchase ads for our first or second issue and receive our Sponsoring Advertisers Rate for the rest of the year! Act now, because rates will change and these will be your only chance to lock yourself into these low prices for the rest of the year.

All ads are produced in b&w/grayscale. Dimensions described below are in inches. All advertisers receive a free copy of each publication their ad appears in, and additional copies by request for half off, plus shipping.

INTRODUCTORY SPONSORING ADVERTISING RATES (for 2014)
Full page (7.75 x 10.5) $250 per issue
Half page tall (3.75 x 10) $175 per issue
Half page wide (7.25 x 5) $175 per issue
Quarter page (3.75 x 5) $65.00 per issue
Eighth page (3.75 x 2.5) $35.00 per issue

NORMAL ADVERTISING RATES
Full page (7.75 x 10.5) $350 per issue
Half page tall (3.75 x 10) $200 per issue
Half page wide (7.25 x 5) $200 per issue
Quarter page (3.75 x 5) $95.00 per issue
Eighth page (3.75 x 2.5) $45.00 per issue

Space will be reserved once payment has been received/cleared. Ads are due one month prior to issue release dates (see below) and payment is due at that time (if not sent prior); non-payment in a timely manner will result in the ad not running. Paying advertisers that miss the ad artwork deadline will be bumped to the following issue. An electronic proof of the ad will be sent to advertisers prior to printing the magazine. Timely response via e-mail is appreciated. A non-response is assumed to be agreement that there are no errors/issues.

PUBLISHING SCHEDULE FOR *THE ACT ITSELF*

Vol 1, Issue 1 - April 30, 2014 - Ads and payment due April 1, 2014
Vol 1, Issue 2 - August 31, 2014 - Ads and payment due August 1, 2014
Vol 1, Issue 3 - December 31, 2014 - Ads and payment due December 1, 2014

Term and Conditions

Advertisers using PO Box number in their address must furnish Publisher with a legal street address and phone number. No cancellations accepted after deadline.

Payments (US funds only) can be made via PayPal, check or Money Order. For details on how to make paayment, please contact:

John Teehan
Managing Editor, *The Act Itself*
info@theactitself.com

Electronic File Requirements

Images (minimum 300 dpi .psd, .tif, or .eps); PDF (fonts imbedded); Files must be sent electronically. For questions or troubleshooting, contact info@theactitself.com.

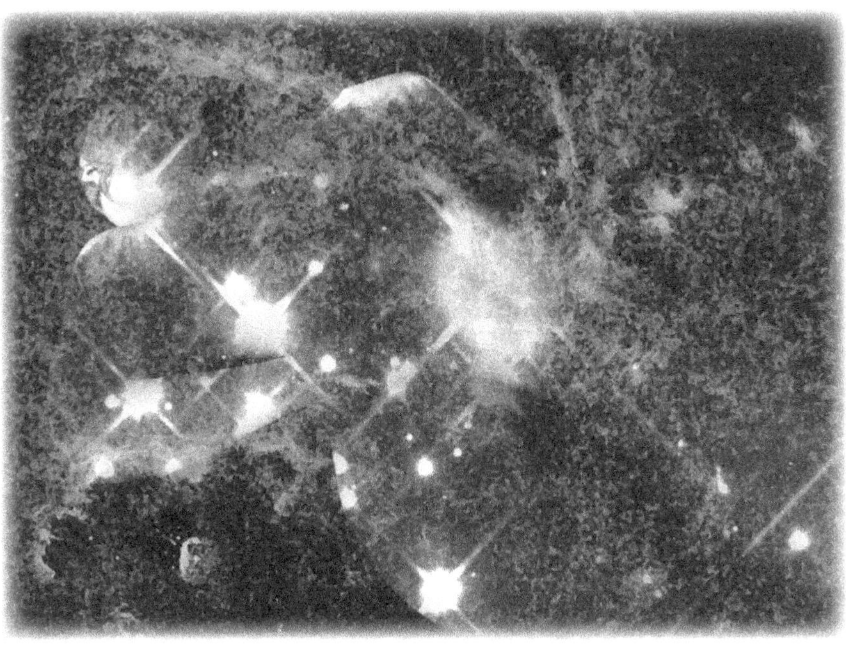

Christopher Chamberlain is a professional artist who earns his living through the artwork that he creates. Many of those pieces tend to be of the erotic variety, and comics are a close second. While his artwork has been displayed in galleries across the world, you can see some of his work at manyfacesart.blogspot.com.

BACK DOWN SOUTH

by Donnie Magazino

"How about some Oklahoma cheese grits?" I ask Melanie on the other side of my bed. I'm joking, making fun of her southern twang.

She smiles, crinkles her adorable little nose, then rolls back over to sleep.

I had forgotten that she wasn't a morning person. So I drift into my office, hoping to get some work done before the southern belle wakes up and makes breakfast. But my Scarlett O'Hara has other plans.

I feel her naughty hands roping around my waist and tickling me seconds after I settle into my chair.

"Good morning, sweetie," she groans, still half asleep.

"Honey, I'm trying to get some work done."

I try to unlace myself from her grip, but she's persistent.

"Uhhh-uhh, I need you back in the bedroom for a minute, love," she rasps in the sassy drawl.

"Baby, I can't. I really need to finish this..."

She kisses my neck, softly, warmly.

"I'm feeling homesick, honey. Need to take a trip down south..."

Her kisses get hotter and travel closer to the border.

"... but I simply have to get this done..." I answer.

But she's fast approaching the Mason-Dixon line.

"... It's a very important..."

She kisses her way down to Missouri.

"... report that needs to be done..."

She dips eastward to northern Florida.

"... um... uh..."

Takes a swing through Alabama.

"... and it's also important..."

Nibbles her way through Mississippi.

"um... you see..."

Makes some lovely slurps in Louisiana.

"... and I really need to..."

She reaches the southern tip of Texas.

"You know what? Work can wait!" I decide, tossing her over my shoulder and carrying her into the bedroom.

"Carry me back to Old Virginia," I croon.

I throw her onto the bed and she greets me with a hungry stare.

"You," Jason told him, "get this man a towel, preferably get him any clothes and – "

"I won't wear them," I said.

"What? Why not?"

"I'll just take them off again."

"Honey, this trip is just getting started," she answers, peeling me out of my pajamas.

She tilts a leg up lovingly. An invitation.

I accept, kissing and sucking my way past her knees, to her magnificent thighs and into the castle. She loves it, curving up to meet my kisses, grabbing at my hair, whimpering like a wounded poodle.

But now it's her turn. She gives her full lips a lick and guides my throbbing meat into that wonderful mouth. She sucks, licks, caresses me into an impossible state of arousal. Her reddish-brown nest blurs into a lovely crown. I can't take much more.

But she has much more to give. She guides my stone-hard cock into the palace and we both gasp for a second. I grind my hips, slowly at first, but she urges me into harder, stronger thrusts with her eyes, with her hips, with her strong legs.

I push harder, heavier. She loves it. Now her ankles are on my shoulders and I pick up speed and intensity.

"Harder, darling, harder!" she screams.

I watch her pretty face curl into a beautiful mess and it pushes me into harder, faster pumps. Her voice floats into a higher octave. Her hips greet mine halfway and make a loud, happy crash. I push until her nails dig into my back and her kisses get clumsy and almost angry.

I can feel us both rising and rising, her breasts meeting my chest, her legs curling around my waist, her face and hair and arms flailing wildly and out of control.

Then we fall, out of breath and too tired for words.

I am spent, nothing left but my racing heart. But I can't go back to sleep just yet. Right now I have to figure out how to make Oklahoma Cheese grits.

Donnie Magazino is a writer of erotica whose work has appeared in Clean Sheets, The Erotic Woman, Oysters & Chocolate *and* For The Girls. *His alto ego lives in Minneapolis and is putting together a web series called* Adventures in WilliamWorld *(Look for it on YouTube).*

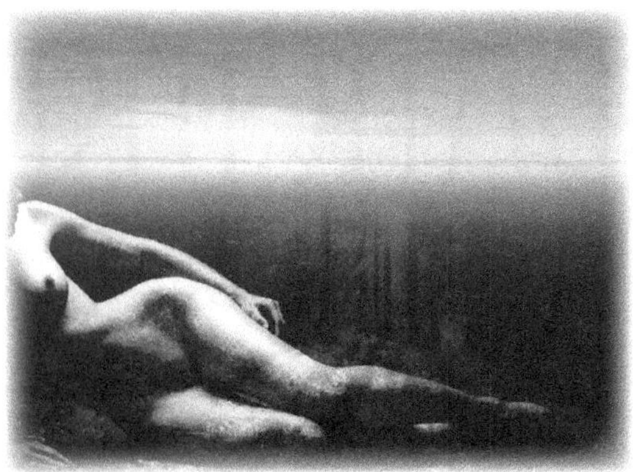

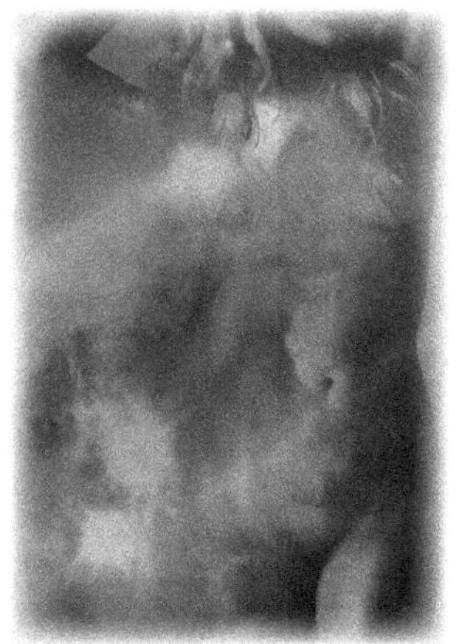

LADY POKINGHAM, or THEY ALL DO IT

Giving an Account of Her Luxurious Adventures – Both Before and after Her Marriage with Lord Crim-Con, PART IV

by Anonymous

(printed for the Society of Vice, 1880)

(Continued.)

My partner was far too impetuous to heed my faint remonstrances, and in spite of all I could do to keep my thighs closed his venturesome hand soon took possession of my heated cunny. "If I die I must have you, darling lady," he whispered in my ear, as he suddenly forced me quite back on the sofa, and tried to raise my clothes.

"Ah! No! No! I shall faint. How your violence frightens me!" I sighed, trying to smother my desires by simulating helplessness, and then feigning unconsciousness I promised myself a rare treat by allowing him to think I really had fainted, which, no doubt, would urge him to take advantage of the moment to riot unrestrained in the enjoyment of my most secret charms.

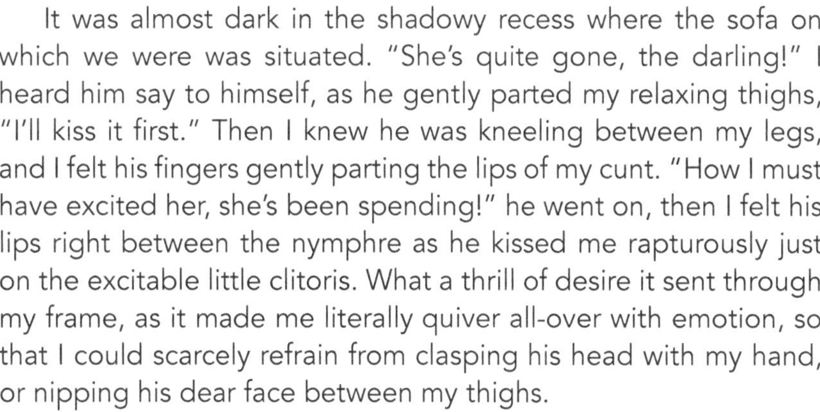

It was almost dark in the shadowy recess where the sofa on which we were was situated. "She's quite gone, the darling!" I heard him say to himself, as he gently parted my relaxing thighs, "I'll kiss it first." Then I knew he was kneeling between my legs, and I felt his fingers gently parting the lips of my cunt. "How I must have excited her, she's been spending!" he went on, then I felt his lips right between the nymphre as he kissed me rapturously just on the excitable little clitoris. What a thrill of desire it sent through my frame, as it made me literally quiver all-over with emotion, so that I could scarcely refrain from clasping his head with my hand, or nipping his dear face between my thighs.

This only lasted a few moments, which seemed awfully long in my excitable state, my cunt was spending and throbbing under the voluptuous titillations of his velvety tongue. Heavens how I wanted to feel his prick inside of me! and could not have feigned my fainting state another instant, but the moment my lips were in the act of parting to implore him to fuck me at once he started to his feet, pushing my thighs as wide apart as possible, and directly I felt the hot head of his cock placed to the mark; slowly and gradually he pushed his way in, as contracting my usually tight affair I made it as difficult as I could for him to achieve possession. How he kissed my lips, calling me, "Darling lady, dear Beatrice, oh, you love, what pleasure you give me!"

I felt him spend a torrent of his warm essence right up to my vitals, and then lay still upon me exhausted for the moment by the profuseness of his emission.

Still apparently in the state of inanimation, and without opening my eyes, I made my cunt nip and contract on his throbbing prick as it was soaking within me, in such a manner that he was almost immediately aroused from his delicious lethargy, and recommenced his movements, exclaiming to himself, What a love of a girl, even in her fainting state, the love pressure of her cunt responds to the action of my prick. What pleasure it would be if I could but arouse her to sensibility!" as he kissed me over and over again rapturously, quickening his stroke till my blood was so fired I could no longer impose upon him, so I suddenly threw my arms around the dear boy's neck, whilst my amorous kisses responding to his silently assured him of the delight he was affording me.

"Here they are, the sly things, why Beatrice is the hottest of the lot, see she has got Charles well in her," laughed Lady Bertha; bringing a light into the room, and followed by all the others, looking very excited, and as if some of them at least had been doing the same; in fact I could see the front of John's trousers were undone, whilst the flushed face of Lady Montairy, and the delighted manner in which she clung to the handsome young French page, assured me that she at least was on the best of terms with her partner, added to which, in the background, Bridget and Fanny seemed as loving as any of them from their damask cheeks and sparkling eyes.

Charles was dreadfully confused, and I felt that the surprise was taking all the vigour out of him, so with the greatest presence of mind, I threw my legs over his buttocks and embraced him more firmly than ever, as I exclaimed, "It's this naughty fellow, my dear, has taken liberties with me, that I fainted from fear, and he is in complete possession of my virginity, and having aroused all my passions to the highest pitch he wants to withdraw, slap his bottom well for me, and make him now complete my pleasure, after satisfying his own greedy lustfulness!"

He struggled hard to get away but I held him tightly, whilst all of them slapped him without mercy, making him fairly bound in the saddle to my great delight, more especially when I soon found him swelling up quite an unnatural stiffness, till his prick was almost breaking my quim, and he was furiously fucking with all his might, as he cried out for them to leave off and let him do it properly.

The noise of the slaps on his bum seemed to give me intense delight and I never remember to have had a more delicious fucking, which as he had spent twice previously lasted a long good bout, till we both came together almost frantic with delight, as our mutual essences were commingled at the same moment.

"There, don't let me catch any two of you slipping away by themselves again," said Lady Montairy, as she gave a last tremendous slap, which fairly made the poor fellow bound under her hand, in spite of his exhaustive spend. "It spoils

The noise of the slaps on his bum seemed to give me intense delight and I never remember to have had a more delicious fucking, which as he had spent twice previously lasted a long good bout, till we both came together almost frantic with delight, as our mutual essences were commingled at the same moment.

half the fun, when some are so sly, and pretend to be mock-modest when at the same time they are quite or more inclined for the sport than anyone."

All returned to the drawing-room and refreshed ourselves with champagne, jellies and other reinvigorating delicacies, as we laughed and bantered the four young fellows and the two lady's-maids about their sweethearts and love experiences, till Bertha wrote all the names of the female members of our party on slips of paper, which she said she would hold for the boys to draw their prizes, declaring that Bridget and Fanny, if drawn, should submit to be fucked, although they protested their virginity and determination to keep it for the present, much as they enjoyed the other fun.

First of all she asked us to assist her in stripping our cavaliers quite naked, in order that we might enjoy the sight of their adolescent beauties (John, the eldest, being only nineteen). They were finely formed young fellows, but the splendid proportions of Master Charlie's penis carried off the honours of the evening, being more than eight inches long and very thick. My lady friends were in ecstasies at the sight, and almost made the other three young fellows jealous by each wishing he might draw them for a partner.

"Now there shall be no deception or cheating; I've a novel idea how the lots shall be drawn," said Bertha, drawing up her clothes till she showed the beautiful lips of her luscious cunt, just peeping out between the slit in her drawers as her legs were wide apart; then drawing me close to her side she gave me the slips of paper and whispered in my ear to arrange them in her cunt with the seven ends just sticking out. It was soon done, then our gentlemen had to kneel down in front and each one drew his paper with his mouth.

This was a jolly bit of fun, Bertha looked as if she would have liked to be fucked by all four instead of merely having them draw lots from her gap, which was so tickled as they drew out the papers that she actually spent under the novel excitement.

John drew Bridget; James, Lady Montairy; Charles, Bertha, whilst I was lucky enough to get the handsome Lucien, who had been eyeing me with a most amorous leer, which you may be sure did not in the least offend me.

Corisande and Fanny were told to fit themselves with a couple of most artistically moulded india-rubber dildoes of a very natural size and not too large, which Lady St. Aldegonde said her husband had procured for the purpose of having his lady bottom-fuck himself occasionally, when he wanted extra stimulation. "And now my dear, they will be very useful in enabling you to give these nice youths the double pleasure as they enjoy their partners."

The ladies were now also divested of everything, till the complete party were in a state of buff, excepting the pretty boots and stockings, which I always think look far sweeter than naked legs and feet.

The interest centred in the engagement between Bertha and Charles, as the others were all anxious to see the working of his fine prick in her splendid cunt. He was in a very rampant state of anticipation, so she laid him at full length on his back, on a soft springy couch, then stretching across his legs she first bent down her head to kiss and lubricate the fine prick with her mouth, then placing herself right over him gradually sheathed his grand instrument within her longing cunt, pressing down upon him, with her lips glued to his, as she seemed to enjoy the sense of possessing it all. I motioned to her bottom with my finger, and Fanny, understanding my ideas, at once mounted up behind her mistress and brought the head of her well-cold-creamed dildoe to the charge against her brown-wrinkled bottom-hole, at the same time clasping her hands round Bertha, one hand feeling Charlie's fine prick, whilst the fingers of her other were tickling the fine clitoris of our mistress of the ceremonies. It was a delightful tableau, and it awfully excited us all when they at once plunged into a course of most delicious fucking. Fanny was as excited as either of them as she vigorously dildoed her mistress, and kept her hands stimulating them in front. Corisande now attacked Fanny behind with her dildoe, delighting her with frigging combined.

How they screamed with delight, and spent over and over again; it is impossible to describe, but I had got Lucien's fine prick in my hand as we were kissing and indulging in every possible caress. It throbbed in my grasp as I repeatedly drew back the foreskin, till at length fearing he would spend over my hand, I sank back on a sofa, and drew him upon me, guiding his affair to my longing cunt, whilst he clasped me round the body and kissed more ardently than ever. I could see all that was going on round the room, Lady Bertha still riding furiously on Charles, stimulated by the double exertions of Fanny and Corisande, and watched with delight the frenzied enjoyment of the lady's-maid, as she handled and felt how Charles was going on in front, whilst her

It throbbed in my grasp as I repeatedly drew back the foreskin, till at length fearing he would spend over my hand...

young mistress's dildoe almost drove her to distraction by its exciting movements in her bottom. Lady Montairy was riding James as he sat on a chair, but John was being quite baffled by his partner Bridget, who wriggled and avoided every attempt of his cock to get into her, as she kissed and allowed him any liberty except the last favour of love.

At last we all finished. "Now," said Lady Bertha, "we will rest and refresh ourselves a little, and then we will see to Bridget and Fanny having their maidenheads properly taken; meanwhile I will tell you a little adventure I once had down at Brentham a few months after my marriage. Well, you must know St. Aldegonde wanted to represent the county in parliament, and a general election was expected very soon, indeed it was rumoured the dissolution would occur almost immediately, so no time was to be lost, and there was one great landowner, who if we could but secure him to our side we were sure of carrying the day. He had been an old admirer of mine, and had been much chagrined at my lordship's success in obtaining my hand, and we both knew he was almost certain to throw all his influence into the opposite scale. We were just going to bed one night, and about to fall asleep after a beautiful fuck (it is nice when first married) when a sudden idea made me quite laugh, it seemed so good.

"St. Aldegonde was quite anxious to know what I had been thinking of, 'My love,' I said, kissing him (I don't often do that now, except when I want to wheedle him out of something) would you mind giving a bit of my cunt to secure your return for the county?' 'Why, Bertha darling, just at this moment nothing would make me jealous, as you've sucked the last drop of spend from my cock,' he said, with a yawn, and then realising my idea, he continued, 'Do you mean Mr. Stiffington, my love; it's a bright idea, if you do, and damned cheap way of buying him, besides cunt could never be reckoned bribery.'

"The prospect of adventure, added to the good I might do for my husband, made me volunteer to do it, and as secrecy was everything, we determined that I should go down to Brentham disguised as a servant.

"Next day we started apparently to go to Paris, but I left St. Aldegonde at the railway station, and started off to Brentham by myself after changing my dress at a hotel. The housekeeper at Brentham was the only person whom I took into my confidence, but of course she did not know all.

"She passed me off as a niece from town, who had a holiday for a few days, and I mixed with the servants as one of themselves; the idea that I could be Lady Bertha never entered their heads, as I was supposed to be gone abroad for a tour.

"Without delay she got the coachmen to drive me over to Mr. Stiffington's place, Manly Hall, with a note to that gentleman on some special business, which I must deliver with my own hands.

"The gentleman was at home, and I was soon ushered into the library, where he was attending to his letters or other business, after breakfast, about 11 o'clock in the morning.

"'Well, young woman, let me have the particular letter you brought from Brentham; why couldn't a groom have done as messenger? By Jove! you're a nice looking girl though!' he said suddenly, seeming to notice my appearance.

"'If you please, sir,' I said, blushing, 'I'm Lady Bertha's maid, and bring a very important note from Lord St. Aldegonde.'

"He was a fine handsome fellow of about thirty-five, full of life and vigour in every limb; his eyes looked me through and through, then suddenly he penetrated my disguise, as he exclaimed, 'Ah, no, you're Lady Bertha herself. What is the cause of this mystery?'

"I was all confusion, but he told me to sit down and tell him without reserve what I wanted, as he drew to a sofa and seated himself by my side.

'"Your vote and interest to secure my husband's return for the county,' I said in a low voice, 'we know you can turn the scale, so I ventured to solicit your influence in person.'

"But how can you expect me to be otherwise than hostile to a man who deprived me of your beautiful self,' he replied, 'why did you jilt me for a lordling?'

"I looked down in pretended distress, as I answered with an almost inaudible voice, 'If you only knew our family necessities, it would soothe your wounded self-respect, nothing but his dukedom in perspective sealed my fate against my own feeble will, and now it is my duty to further his interests in every way.'

"'Dear Bertha,' he exclaimed excitedly, 'do I really hear right, would you have preferred me, can you not pity my unrequited love, won't you even favour me with a smile as I look in your face?' taking my hand and covering it with impassioned kisses. 'I would support your husband, but—but I must be bribed—let me think what you shall give me, dearest; of course he's had your first virginity, but I must have the second, it will cost him nothing, and no one need know.'

"He was growing quite impetuous; with one arm around my waist, whilst he covered my blushing face with the most ardent kisses, I could feel his other hand wandering over my bosom or my thighs, as he felt them through my dress, then taking one of my hands he forced me to feel his standing cock which he had let out of his breeches; the mere touch sent a thrill of desire through my whole frame as I sank backwards in an assumed faint.

"He jumped up, fastened the door, then went to a drawer, from which he took a small book and a little box, then kneeling down by my side he gently raised my clothes, kissing my legs all the way up, inside or outside of my drawers as he could get at them, and parting my thighs opened the slit in my drawers, till he had a fair view of my pussey. 'What a sweet little slit, what soft silky down it is ornamented with,' I could hear him say as he pressed his lips to my Mons Veneris, then I could feel his fingers parting the lips of my cunt with the greatest tenderness to enable him to kiss the little button of love. This was too much, I pressed his head down with my hands, as I spent over his tongue with a deep drawn sign of pleasure. 'She's mine, how she likes it, the touches of my tongue have made her come!'

"'Look, darling,' he continued, as he rose to his feet, 'I

Keeping my clothes up, and making me retain hold of his priapus in one hand, he showed me a series of splendid little drawings in the book, all illustrating the way to enjoy bottom-fucking.

thought a few delicate kisses would revive you if properly bestowed in the most sensitive place, but I don't mean to have you there; this book will show you the most delightful avenue of bliss, and open up to your ravished senses heavenly bliss you have hither had no conception of.'

"Keeping my clothes up, and making me retain hold of his priapus in one hand, he showed me a series of splendid little drawings in the book, all illustrating the way to enjoy bottom-fucking. He could see I was tremendously excited, so lost no time in placing me on my hands and knees on the sofa, then anointing my tight little bum-hole with some ointment from the box, and putting some also on the shaft of his prick, he made me push my bottom well out behind, with my legs wide apart so as to give him every facility, but 'Ah! Ah! No, no, I can't bear it!' I exclaimed, the tears fairly starting to my eyes as I felt the first advance of his lovely engine, forcing its way through the tightened orifice; the pain was like a number of needles pricking the part all at once. I can describe the sensation as the sphincter muscle gradually relaxed in no other way. He frigged me deliciously in front all the while, pushing so firmly and getting in in such a gentle manner behind that I seemed to love him more and more every moment, and long for him to accomplish his task, and complete my enjoyment, as the very pain seemed a percursor to some extraordinary bliss, nor was I disappointed; the pain was soon succeeded by the most delicious sensations as his movements stirred me up to the highest pitch of excitement, and he never withdrew till we had spent thrice in rapturous ecstasies, screaming with delight and almost losing our lives from excess of enjoyment.

"Thus my mission was successful, and his lordship became a Member of Parliament."

This tale had worked us all up, so that we were mutually groping each other's privates, and as soon as Bertha had finished we seized Fanny and Bridget, but too much of the same thing being rather tedious to read I will only say that John and Charles took their virginities in splendid style, when the girls really found no more nonsense would be tolerated.

This was my last adventure in town, and in the next part I shall go on to relate what happened after my marriage with Lord Crim-Con, which took place shortly afterwards.

(To be continued.)

Merry Blacksmith
Studio
Fine Art

www.ingramcontent.com/pod-product-compliance
Lightning Source LLC
LaVergne TN
LVHW061247100826
845148LV00008B/1050

* 9 7 8 1 5 9 3 9 3 3 9 8 2 *